All at once, I felt a blast of icy air sweep over me. I had the eerie feeling that someone was in the room with me now. I'd had the same feeling in the little room before. But this time the feeling was so strong that I actually took a step back.

I whispered, "What do you want? Tell me! Please, tell me!"

LITTLE ROOM OF
TERROR

by Laurie Lykken

cover illustration Richard Kriegler

This book is for Karisha Bruechner—
May you always believe in yourself!

Published by Willowisp Press, Inc.
10100 SBF Drive, Pinellas Park, Florida 34666

Copyright © 1991 by Willowisp Press, Inc.

Printed in the United States of America

10 9 8 7 6 5 4 3 2 1

ISBN 0-87406-538-0

One

"WELL, Diane," Dad said as he pulled our car into a gas station, "we're almost home now."

"Home?" I repeated the word doubtfully. As far as I was concerned, home was what I'd left two hours earlier. Home wasn't where I was going now.

"Yes, home," Dad said firmly. "You've got to start thinking of this move as a new beginning. It'll make everything easier for you...for all four of us."

Besides me and him, Dad was talking about his new wife, Peggy, and Peggy's eight-year-old daughter, Lisa. We were all going to live together, and I was supposed to be happy about it. I guess it was supposed to be no big deal, leaving Gran and the house she'd shared with Dad and me after Mom died.

I bit my tongue not to say anything as Dad

parked by one of the gas pumps. He told the attendant to fill the tank and we got out of the car. It felt good to stretch my legs.

"Come on. Let's find a vending machine and get something cold to drink," said Dad. Reaching over, he mussed my short, brown hair the way he had when I was little. I'm twelve now, but he still does things like that.

"What'll it be, Diane?" Dad asked. We'd found a machine and he was digging change out of his pocket. I mumbled that an orange drink would be fine, and he got one for each of us.

"You're going to like the house, you know," Dad said suddenly. "It's very interesting."

I hadn't seen the house Dad and Peggy had bought in Edmonton yet. And actually, I didn't much care. It's not that I had anything against Edmonton. I just didn't want to move there. I liked living in Springfield with Gran and I knew I'd miss her like crazy. I also had friends there that I didn't want to leave, like my best friend, Whitney. I'd told Dad all that, but he hadn't listened to me. Or, if he had, he hadn't cared enough about my feelings to do anything about them.

"You know," Dad continued, "both Peggy and Lisa are really anxious to see you, honey. In fact, you're practically all Lisa talks about since she returned from visiting her father in California."

"If they're so anxious to see me, then why didn't Peggy and Lisa come with you to pick me up?" I asked.

"Well, Peggy and I did consider all of us coming for the trip," Dad admitted, "but Peggy didn't want to leave the house unattended."

"But it would have only been overnight," I said. Then I frowned. "Is there a lot of crime in Edmonton or something? Is that why she didn't want to leave the house?"

"No, nothing like that," Dad said quickly. He finished off his orange drink in one big swallow, then crushed the can and tossed it in a litter bin.

I polished mine off, too. We began to walk back to the car. "So what's the deal, Dad?" I persisted. "Are there problems with the neighbors? Is that it?"

"Not exactly," said Dad. Then he sighed. He glanced at me for a second. "It's just that, well...there's this old woman in our neighborhood who's been giving Peggy a hard time ever since she found out that we were *planning* to buy the house. That means even before the wedding. The old woman comes around—all the time, it seems—and she just stands by the house and stares up at it. She stands there and stares, and mumbles and points."

"Weird," I said. At least for the moment, Dad and I seemed to be agreeing on something. I waited impatiently while he paid for the gas and started up the car. He eased back into traffic after we'd fastened our seatbelts. We were on our way again.

"So this old woman," I said, "she just hangs around?" This was maybe the only interesting thing Dad had talked about on the drive. I wanted to get him back on the track.

"Yes, and she hasn't let up, either," Dad answered. "If anything, she's become more of a pest than ever lately. Peggy has even spotted her hanging around at night, when it's dark."

Dad peeked over at me, probably to see how I was reacting to this.

"Peggy's tried everything to discourage this old woman," Dad said, twisting his neck left and right. The drive was getting to him, too. "It sounds ridiculous, but it's a very frustrating situation."

"How weird!" I repeated. I tried to imagine what it must be like to have some stranger always staring and pointing at your house, like you'd done something wrong. "But I don't get it," I continued. "Did this woman want to buy the house for herself or something?"

"No, and that's a big part of the frustration, I'm afraid," said Dad. "Neither Peggy nor I can figure out why she's hanging around. No one seems to know, at least none of the neighbors we've met so far."

Dad paused, then shook his head, as if he were trying to shake the woman from his mind. "I guess she's just old and confused," he said. "And being as strange as she is has made her sort of the town character. No one wants to get very close to her. Anyway, she's made Peggy uneasy about leaving the house totally empty for more than an hour or two at a time, at least until we can get her unwanted visits under control."

"I still don't get it," I told Dad. "If this woman didn't want to buy the house herself, then why does she care that you bought it?" *Also*, I wondered to myself, *if this woman was just confused, why was Peggy upset by her?* I looked at Dad. He was looking pretty upset himself by now.

"I'm not explaining it well," Dad said after a moment. "I probably shouldn't have mentioned this woman to you at all. It's just that I wanted you to know that Peggy has been under some unusual strain lately. I guess I'd like to be able to count on you to be cheerful and helpful. How about it, Diane? What do you say? Can you manage to do that for me?"

I slumped a little into my seat. "I guess I don't have much choice," I finally said. "Nothing's going to stay the way I want it, no matter what I say."

Dad cleared his throat, and his voice got a little softer. "After your mom died, I was really happy that we could live with Gran in the house where I grew up. But things change, honey. I'm remarried now. I've found a great new house for all of us to live in, and you belong with me. Besides, you know we'll visit Gran a lot, and she'll visit us, too."

Being with Dad was one thing. I wanted that—at least most of the time. But he wasn't going to convince me that the move was a great thing.

"Diane?" Dad said.

I realized my mind had been wandering. "I guess I was daydreaming," I replied. "But don't worry. I'll do my best to fit in with everyone, and to like the house." I knew it was what he wanted to hear.

"Good," Dad said. He pulled into the left lane to pass a truck. As he moved back into the right lane, he said, "And let's not mention that we talked about the old woman who comes around. There's no point in getting Peggy needlessly upset. Right?"

"I guess," I said, shrugging. "I won't say anything. It's not that big of a deal."

I tried to make it sound like I was getting bored by the whole conversation. But the truth was, if there was anything at all interesting about this move, it might be that weird old lady.

I admit it. I was curious. I wanted to see this old woman for myself. I wanted to see why she made Dad nervous—and why she made Peggy afraid to leave the house for long.

Who was she? I wondered. *And what did she want?*

Two

"THIS is our street," Dad announced. "Dorsey Avenue."

"Is that the house over there?" I pointed at a cheerful-looking, one-and-a-half story house that reminded me a little of Gran's. There were lots of flowers planted out front, and the yard was a pretty shade of green. Living there, I thought, wouldn't be so bad.

"Nope." Dad nodded his head toward the end of the block. "It's that one, *all* the way down at the end."

I saw then that Dorsey Avenue came to a dead end at an overgrown lot. Behind the tangle of a scraggly hedge, I could just barely make out an old wreck of a house.

"That one!" I cried. "You've got to be kidding!" The house was a mess. It even had a loose shutter dangling at a cockeyed angle from one of the windows on the second floor.

"That's it, all right," Dad said proudly. "It's a big, old Victorian mansion. One of the first grand houses in town, in fact. It was built for the first doctor in town and his family. The street—Dorsey Avenue—was named for them. This whole street we're now driving down was once their driveway. It's a genuine historical landmark. Obviously, it needs work, but we got a terrific bargain on it. Imagine that!"

"I can't," I muttered. Dad didn't seem to hear me, though.

Dad turned slowly onto the rocky remains of a driveway. He pulled up just far enough to get the back end of the car out of the street. Then he turned the engine off.

"Fixing the driveway is a ways down the list," he said. He nodded at the house again. "We had to do the roof first. It leaked. Right now we're working on the inside."

It was an oddly shaped house, with several small porches tacked on here and there. That was in addition to the large porch that covered the whole front. There were other rooms jutting out here and there at different levels, too. They all seemed like last-minute ideas and not part of the original house.

Then I noticed that the white paint on the shingles was peeling. More than the one

13

shutter I'd first noticed needed repairing, too. In fact, everything about the house seemed to sag, as if the old place had simply given up even trying to look decent. It gave off a gloomy, sad feeling.

I was still staring at the house in disbelief when the front door burst open and Lisa came flying out. Peggy was right behind her.

"Here's the welcoming committee," Dad said cheerfully as Lisa came skipping across the sagging front porch ahead. She flew down the crumbling front steps, and hurried over to the car just as I stepped out and onto the weed-infested lawn.

"Diane! Diane!" Lisa cried. Her pale, blond braids flew out behind her as she jumped up and down excitedly. "I didn't think you were ever going to get here!" she exclaimed.

"Uh...hi, Lisa," I said. I tried to smile, but it was hard to do a very good job of it with that beat-up, old house on my mind.

"How was your trip, Diane?" Peggy asked.

"Okay," I said, but my mind was on other things. I'd noticed something else odd about the house. Even though there were only a couple of little clouds in the sky, there was absolutely no sun shining in the yard. I turned slowly around and saw that the sun was still shining everywhere else, though. It was like an invisible cloud was hanging over the house and nowhere else. And that made the house seem even spookier than it had before.

"Where is the sun?" I asked Dad.

Dad laughed lightly. "It's here, but hidden behind those two big elms," he explained. He pointed at a pair of scraggly trees bordering the lot. "They shade the house beautifully, don't they?"

"Mmmm," I said, not knowing what else I could say.

Peggy laughed. "Come on," she said. "How about a quick tour of the inside?"

"All right!" Lisa grabbed my hand and started trying to pull me toward the house. "Hurry up, Diane! Your room is the best part."

"Hold on, girls," Dad said. "Let's unload the car while we're at it. There's no sense in going all the way up to Diane's new room empty-handed, is there?"

Lisa giggled and let go of my arm. "No. I guess not." Then everyone hurried around the car to the trunk, and I followed.

"I'll take that little box," Lisa volunteered, reaching into the open trunk.

"Be careful with that," I warned as I watched her snatch the small cardboard box containing my collection of glass figurines. I'd wrapped each one carefully in newspaper, but they were still very fragile. The tiny ears and delicate hands were easily chipped off, ruining the piece altogether.

Lisa's face lit up. "What's in here, Diane?" She bounced the box a little bit. "It isn't very heavy."

I could hear the things inside bumping against each other. "It's my glass collection," I told her. "I collect little glass statues." I reached nervously for the box. But Lisa pulled it away before I could even touch it.

"I'll be careful," Lisa assured me. Then she skipped ahead, not being what I would call careful at all. I was about to go after her, when Dad handed me a larger box. My art supplies were in this one.

"Here you go, Diane," Dad said. "Peggy and I can handle the rest of it."

I took the box. Then I said, "Lisa's not being careful enough with my glass collection."

"She looks like she's doing all right to me," Dad said. But he wasn't even looking at her. If he had been, he would have seen Lisa hop carelessly up the front steps before finally disappearing inside the house. The screen door shut with a loud bang after her. Not waiting for Dad and Peggy to finish dividing up my suitcases, I hurried inside after Lisa, worried about my collection.

16

Once my eyes adjusted to the dim inside light, I spotted Lisa. She was sitting on the arm of a sofa, waiting for the rest of us, I guessed. My box of fragile figurines was balanced on her narrow lap. Seeing that they were safe, I sighed with relief. But then I looked around the living room and that feeling of relief vanished.

"Yeck!" I exclaimed. It definitely looked like the setting for a horror movie.

"It's really ugly, isn't it?" asked Lisa. I had to agree.

The living room walls were covered with an awful gray-and-green wallpaper that reminded me of the mold we'd grown on bread for a science project the year before. Each of the four living room windows was hung with dark red curtains. They were the color of dried blood. The ugly curtains didn't go with the awful wallpaper, unless whoever had picked them had been trying to give the effect of hundreds of squashed toads. Then I noticed the funny smell. My nose started to tickle so much I had to set my box down for a second to rub it with the back of my hand. Finally, I sneezed.

"Bless you," Lisa said, jumping to her feet again. "I sneezed the first time I came in here, too," she said. Then, holding her nose, she added, "I think it's those dusty old curtains."

That's when Peggy and Dad came in.

"An old, childless couple lived in this house for the past several years. They kind of let things go, I'm afraid," Peggy said apologetically when she saw Lisa holding her nose.

"Take those old curtains, for example," Peggy said. She paused, then shook her head in disgust. "I'd have taken those dusty things down to be cleaned except that as soon as we get new ones, we'll just be throwing them out." She glanced at Dad, then said, "We had to leave something up to cover the windows in the meantime."

For the first time since I'd seen the house and been distracted by how awful it looked, I remembered the old woman. *Had those terrible curtains stayed up to keep out her prying eyes?* I wondered. But I didn't ask. I'd promised Dad I wouldn't.

"Where is my room?" I asked instead. I was afraid that if we didn't move along quickly, I wouldn't be able to keep that promise much longer.

"Upstairs," Peggy said.

"You're going to love it!" Lisa promised. She hopped on ahead, bouncing my box up and down again in the process.

"Be careful," I told her irritably.

"I *am* being careful," she retorted. But she wasn't being careful enough for me.

"Your bedroom is at the end of this hall, Diane," Dad said once we were all upstairs.

"My room's right here," Lisa said. She nodded at the first open door. I peeked in and saw a white canopy bed with a blue ruffle over it. There were matching blue curtains on the windows. The white walls had been freshly painted. Sunlight was streaming in and the whole room glowed.

"It's pretty," I said. I used to want a canopy bed like Lisa's. I didn't now, of course. It was too young for me. After all, I wasn't a little kid anymore, as I seemed to have to keep reminding Dad.

The next door we passed was closed. "That's the door to the attic," Lisa explained, still playing the tour guide and still jostling my glass things more than I felt she needed to. She was beginning to get on my nerves.

"And here's your room, sweetie," Dad said when we got to the end of the hall. He set down both suitcases. "Tah-dah!" he exclaimed, throwing open the door.

I looked in and felt my mouth fall open. Whatever I'd been expecting, this wasn't it. It was a big room—too big, really. The word huge came to mind, then the word immense.

My room at Gran's was small, but cozy. This huge room wasn't cozy at all. I felt a wave of homesickness wash over me.

"Go on," Dad urged, probably mistaking my silence for awe. "Look around, Diane."

I stepped through the doorway and stopped, letting my eyes travel around the room. The furniture, what there was of it, had all been painted white in an obvious attempt to make it go together. But it didn't. There was no bedspread on the bed, only a mustard-colored blanket. There weren't any curtains on the windows, either. Unlike Lisa's polished room, mine looked like it had just been thrown together. I hated it.

"It's not finished, of course," Peggy said quickly. I guess she could see my disappointment. "I thought you'd want to choose the colors for your curtains and spread yourself."

Of course, Peggy knew what Lisa liked and didn't like. She didn't know those things about me, though. She'd married my dad, not me. And Dad—well, he'd always left things like decorating to my mom. After she died, Gran sort of took care of things. Dad really had no clue what my tastes were all about. I felt like an outsider. Another wave of homesickness swept over me.

I walked over to the windows, which looked

out on the backyard. At least the sun seemed to be shining out there. Then, suddenly, the sunshine vanished. The sky was clouding up. It was going to rain. The weather seemed just like my feelings, because all at once I felt so sorry for myself, I was sure I was going to cry.

"Look, Diane," I heard Lisa say from somewhere in back of me. "Over here." But I didn't want to look. I didn't want to do anything anyone wanted me to do anymore. I felt I'd given in enough that day. I was getting tired of being ordered around, tired of being made to do things I didn't want to do. Most of all, I was tired of being told to feel a certain way. I wanted to cry, and I wanted to be alone when I did. Then, under all that sadness and self-pity, I felt myself starting to get angry.

"Look over here, Diane," Lisa insisted. "Please, look. This is the best part of your room and the best part of the tour, too."

"Diane's tired, honey," Peggy said sympathetically. "Maybe she'd like to be alone for a while so she can get used to her surroundings. We can finish the tour another time."

"But I want to see her face when she sees her surprise," Lisa whined.

"Let Lisa show you our surprise, Diane. Then we'll go," Dad promised.

"Oh, all right," I said, spinning around.

Anything to get rid of them all, I told myself. All of them, including Dad, were bugging me.

When I turned, I saw that Lisa was standing in front of what looked like a closed closet door. There was a matching door next to it. Both of these doors faced the door to the hall.

"Is this the big surprise?" I asked irritably. "I have *two* closets?"

"Nope," Lisa said. She opened the door next to her. Instead of a closet, I saw stairs. Sunlight cascaded down them from above and pooled on the shiny oak floor around Lisa's white tennis shoes.

"But the clouds..." I said, taking a step toward the open door, drawn to the sunlight. I wondered if I'd been wrong about the stormy clouds I thought I'd seen. Glancing back over my shoulder at the windows, I saw that the sun was shining. Had I imagined those clouds?

"What clouds?" Dad asked. "It isn't supposed to rain today, is it?" Everyone looked toward the window for a second.

"Not until tonight at least," Peggy said.

"Why don't you lead the way upstairs now, Lisa?" Dad suggested. But Lisa's smile faded, and she shook her head.

"I want someone else to go first," she told Dad, sounding even younger than her eight years. I pushed past them both.

"I'll go up first," I said, and I started up.

When I finally reached the top of the stairs, my mouth dropped open. I was in a little round room with a single, large window facing the backyard at the same angle as the two windows in my bedroom. Above my head was a skylight. Chubby, white clouds were drifting directly overhead. They looked as gentle and innocent as sheep in a nursery rhyme. How could I have thought it was about to rain? It was a beautiful day!

"Do you like it?" Lisa asked from behind me. "It's the top room of a tower!"

Dad said, "Your bedroom is actually part of the tower, too."

I hadn't noticed the tower from outside. But then, it had to be on the back side of the house, and I hadn't seen the back of the house from the outside yet. This was the highest room in the house, was my next thought. That meant it was above all the other horrible things about the house. And now that I was in it, I felt like I'd stepped out of all the ugliness below. I knew I was going to be happy up here in my own private world.

"We had the skylight put in when we had the roof done," I heard Dad say. He sounded far away, even though he really wasn't.

"I can draw up here," I said softly, to myself

really. "It'll be my very own art studio."

I heard Dad chuckle. "That was the idea. I'm glad you like it, honey."

"Well, now that we've shown Diane her surprise, I think we should let her get going on her unpacking," Peggy said.

"But I don't want to go," Lisa whined. "I want to stay up here with Diane."

Peggy slipped her arm around Lisa. "I'm sure Diane will let you come back once she's settled in."

I knew right away that everyone expected me to eagerly agree with Peggy. But I just continued to stare out the window at the backyard as if I hadn't even heard her. I didn't want to make any more promises, especially one that I knew I couldn't keep. I had this powerful feeling that as long as I was up in my little tower room by myself, I'd never be lonely again.

Three

"WE'LL be downstairs if you need anything, Diane," Dad said.

"Okay," I said, still looking out the window. I heard the three of them clatter down the stairs. I heard the bedroom door shut. There was a moment of silence. Then I heard a very quiet little "click."

I was finally alone. I sighed with relief. No one was making any demands on me. No one was watching me, wondering how I was reacting to every little thing about the house, to every little word. I stretched out on the bare wood floor beneath my skylight and just watched the clouds float lazily past, not thinking about anything in particular.

I was still daydreaming beneath the skylight, feeling like I was in another world, when I heard the first, gentle knock from below. The second knock was a little louder, a little less gentle. With a sigh, I got up and hurried down-stairs, eager to have whoever it was go away.

"What is it?" I asked through the closed bedroom door.

"We're going grocery shopping." It was Dad. "We want you to take a break and come with us, honey."

"I'll stay here," I called back, still not opening the door. Then I watched the door-knob turn first one way then the other. But the door didn't open.

"Is the door locked?" asked Dad.

That's when I noticed there was a key in the lock. It was an old-fashioned skeleton key, darkened with age. I hadn't noticed it before, but then, I hadn't looked.

"I don't know," I finally answered. "Maybe." I thought of the click I'd heard after Dad and the others left my room. Could that have been the sound of the lock slipping into place?

"Well, *unlock* it, please," Dad said. "I want to come in." I heard a slight edge to Dad's voice.

I called out, "Okay," and turned the key. The lock made the same clicking noise I remembered hearing before. I opened the door.

Dad looked down at the key. "Where did you find that?" he asked.

I shrugged. "It was here in the door."

"That's odd. The Biddles—the people who used to own the house—told us all the keys to the various doors were missing," he commented.

I shrugged. "Not this one," I said.

"No, I guess not. But I'd rather you didn't use it," Dad said.

"Why not?" I asked.

"Everything around this house is so old and neglected that things don't always work right," Dad said. "I don't want you locked in here, unable to get out. That would be dangerous."

"Dangerous," I repeated thoughtfully. But I wasn't thinking about being locked in. I was thinking about locking all of them out. With this key, I could do that. The thought made me feel kind of important.

"Well, come on. Let's go. Peggy and Lisa are waiting for us," Dad said.

"I really don't want to go," I said, "but thanks anyway."

"You have to come," Dad insisted. "We're going to do the shopping for the whole week now and we need your input. You can finish unpacking later."

"I'm not a fussy eater," I said. "Anything the rest of you decide on will be fine with me." I hadn't even started unpacking yet, but I didn't tell Dad that.

Dad frowned and shook his head. "Peggy won't like the idea of you staying here alone, I'm afraid. And I'm not sure I like the idea, either."

"Dad!" I cried, planting my hands firmly on my hips. "I'm 12 years old! I've been baby-sitting other kids since my birthday. What could possibly happen to me while you're gone that I wouldn't be able to handle?"

"Well...," he said hesitantly. He ran his hand through his thick, dark, brown hair and looked quickly down the hall. Then, taking a deep breath, he said, "It's that old woman I told you about, the one who's been bothering Peggy. She just might show up while we're gone. I don't want you to have to deal with her alone."

"Isn't she harmless?" I asked. "That is what you said, isn't it?"

Dad seemed to consider this. Then he sighed. "Okay, Diane. You win. I guess you can stay and unpack. It does make sense in a way. Just don't answer the phone or the door until we get back. Okay? I do think she's a harmless old soul. At least she has been so far. But I don't want to take any chances."

"Okay, Dad," I agreed. "I understand."

"We'll be back in an hour or so," Dad said.

"Meanwhile, leave your bedroom door unlocked, okay? Getting locked in here, especially with no one home, could be dangerous."

After Dad left, I started unpacking my collection of glass figures. No thanks to Lisa, nothing was broken or damaged. I was glad I'd packed my pieces as carefully as I had, or I wouldn't have had a collection anymore. I heard Dad's car start up and drive off just as I unwrapped my favorite piece.

It was a white china goose girl. Gran had a collection of glass figures, too, and the goose girl had always been her favorite. She knew it was my favorite, too. That's why she'd given it to me as a going-away present when Dad and I packed to leave.

I set the goose girl carefully down on the top shelf where I could see it every time I came into my room. Then I turned back to my box of figurines. I had just pulled out my clear glass rabbit when the doorbell rang.

I knew I shouldn't even go downstairs. I'd promised my father I wouldn't open the door, and I wasn't about to break my promise. But when the doorbell rang a second time, I couldn't help myself. I had to see if it was the old woman. I wanted to at least see what she looked like. I charged out of my room. The doorbell rang for a third time as I hurried down the stairs.

Instead of going to the door, though, I went slyly to the front window. Slowly, I pulled the heavy, red curtain back slightly and looked out. But instead of the old woman, I saw a girl. She looked like she was probably my age. She had shoulder-length brown hair, a tiny bit lighter than my own brown hair. Her eyes were blue instead of brown like mine. She looked friendly and nice.

I considered opening the door for her. But while I was still trying to decide what to do, she took a step back and looked up at the house. Then she turned and hurried away. Maybe the place made her as nervous as it made me. I wanted to throw open the door and call after her, but I didn't.

I started to go back up to my room. But just as I started up the stairs to the second floor, I changed my mind. I decided instead to go outside and look around the yard. I hoped the girl who'd come to the door might be out there somewhere. If she was, I decided to tell her I'd been unpacking when she rang the bell and didn't get downstairs until she was already leaving.

I walked through the dining room and into the kitchen. This was a part of the house I hadn't seen yet. But it didn't interest me much at the moment. I was more interested in getting outside, and I quickly found the back door and went out.

The sun was beating down on the backyard. No one was around. I sat down in the tall grass, disappointed, and took a look at the house— the first I'd seen it from the backyard. When I spotted the tower, I let my gaze travel slowly upward. But before I was done examining it, I heard a rustling noise behind me.

Hoping it was the girl, I turned my head quickly, ready to say hello. What I saw instead, however, was a pair of funny black shoes that laced up the front and had chunky-looking heels. They were definitely old lady shoes!

"It's starting," an old, unsteady voice announced. "Just as I knew it would."

I scrambled to my feet, knowing without a shadow of a doubt that this was the old woman who'd been giving Peggy the creeps.

"Who are you, and what do you want?" I asked the old woman. She had gray hair and more wrinkles than I'd ever seen on anyone.

But she didn't answer me. She wasn't even looking at me. She was looking up at the house and didn't seem to even know I was there.

"Who are you?" I asked again in almost a whisper. I carefully inched away to put some distance between us.

But she still didn't answer my question. Instead, the old woman slowly lifted a twisted, knobby finger and pointed at the house.

"Up there," she commanded. "See."

I wanted to tell her no. But for some reason, I couldn't. I didn't understand it, but I felt like I had no choice but to look where she was pointing. And when I did, I saw a strange, bluish glow radiating out of the window in my little room at the top of the tower. I felt my heart jump.

"It's *you!*" the old woman hissed. "I *knew* there would be someone like you!" She sounded more scared than evil, and that frightened me more than anything else about her.

"Me?" I repeated, my voice a squeak. I was still looking at the window, still seeing that bluish glow coming out of it. "What about me?" I asked. I managed to tear my eyes from the window to look at the old woman again. She was staring at me hard. Her eyes were an icy shade of blue. She seemed to be looking right into me. I shuddered, wanting to look away but somehow unable to. Finally, she shook her head and sighed.

"I told her," the old woman said sadly. "I warned her. But she wouldn't listen to me. No one has ever listened to me. They think

I don't know, but I do." Her eyes flashed again. "Be careful," she said to me then. "You *must* be careful now, before it's too late."

"Too late for what?" I asked. "What is that up there? Do you know? Tell me what you know! I'll listen to you. I promise."

"You must stay out of that room," she said, her scratchy voice insistent.

"The tower room!" I gasped. "But that's my little room. Why should I stay out of there? Why?"

I could see by the look the old woman was giving me that she was as frightened of me as I was of her! She also seemed to know that she was asking too much of me. I couldn't give up my little room. It was all I had now, absolutely all.

"Are you going to tell me why?" I demanded as she continued staring at me suspiciously.

"Would it matter if I did?" she asked. Then she shook her head. "I don't think it would."

"It might," I said.

But before she could do anything more than part her thin, dry lips, a car pulled noisily into the driveway and stopped. Dad and the others were back. Already, the old lady was hurrying away.

Four

"HEY, you!" Peggy yelled, leaping out of the car and charging across the lawn toward the retreating woman. "Stop! I want to talk to you!"

But the old woman was already pushing her way through a thin spot in the hedge, and she didn't stop. It was clear that she was running away from Peggy. Once the old woman was out of the yard, Peggy gave up her chase.

I thought again of what the old woman had said. "Stay out of the tower room," she'd told me. But why?

"Are you all right, Diane?" Dad asked.

I nodded. "I'm fine. That was her, wasn't it, Dad?"

Dad nodded. "I'm afraid so. You didn't encourage her, did you?"

"No," I said. "I didn't do anything. I just came outside for a minute, and there she was.

I wouldn't have come out if I'd known she was out here. I swear."

"It's okay," Dad said. "I'm not blaming you."

"Who was that?" Lisa asked, looking from her mother to my father and then back at her mother again. She looked frightened, probably more from Peggy's reaction than anything else, I decided.

"No one," Peggy answered crossly before either Dad or I could say anything.

Dad gave Peggy a funny look. Peggy threw up her hands and said, "Okay. I suppose you're right, Ron. Tell them, then." Peggy's expression seemed to add, "But don't tell them everything."

"That old woman keeps coming over even though we've asked her not to," Dad explained, looking at Lisa. "And that's why your mother wanted to talk to her. You see, older people get a little confused sometimes. They get a notion and hold on to it, no matter how silly or strange that notion is. This poor old woman is one of those people, I'm afraid."

"What kind of a notion does she have?" I asked. "What's she confused about?"

"Things," Peggy said vaguely. I could tell my questions had made her even more uncomfortable than she already was. I decided not to press it.

"She was creepy," Lisa declared with a shudder. "I hope she won't ever come back here again."

With her eyes on Dad, Peggy muttered, "Lisa's right, you know. These visits have got to stop, Ron. I told you she just hangs around here waiting for a chance to pounce. And now you've seen it for yourself."

Dad sighed. "If she comes back again, I'll call the police," he promised. "But she's gone now, and maybe she won't come back again. Now let's bring in the groceries and start dinner. I'm starved."

Then it was Peggy's turn to sigh. But she nodded her head and let Dad lead the way back to the car. Lisa trailed after them. I stayed where I was another moment, looking up at the tower room window. *What*, I wondered, *had caused the pulsing blue light I'd seen? And why did that old woman tell me to stay out of there?* I was pretty sure Peggy and Dad wouldn't want to talk about it with me. But who else could I ask? The old woman herself? Peggy and Dad would never go for that! I finally gave up trying to figure it out and followed the others inside.

As we unloaded the groceries, no one said anything more than, "Where does this go?" or "What's this?" After all the excitement over the old woman being in the yard, the quiet was soothing. In fact, I almost forgot about the old woman and her warning as I scurried around the kitchen, learning where everything was kept.

Finally, Dad went outside to start a charcoal fire for hamburgers. Peggy went along to keep him company. On their way out, they asked Lisa and me to make a tossed salad.

"Is this really the first time you've seen that old woman?" I asked Lisa. Now that we were alone, I couldn't resist finding out what Lisa might know.

Lisa nodded. "She was weird, wasn't she?"

"I guess so," I said. "But maybe she isn't as bad as she looks."

I took a tomato and some lettuce out of the refrigerator and set them down on the cutting board by the sink. I wanted to know more about that old woman. But Lisa didn't seem to know much more than I did.

I picked up the paring knife and began slicing the tomato into wedges for the salad. As far as I was concerned, I was through talking to Lisa about the old woman. Unfortunately, Lisa didn't see things the way I did.

"I wonder why Mom got so mad when she saw her here?" Lisa said. She was kneeling on a stool, her spindly legs tucked under her like some long-legged bird.

I shrugged. "I don't know. I was hoping you knew. But since you don't, let's just drop it and make the salad. Why don't you get the wooden salad bowl your mom said we should use, while I finish slicing this tomato. Okay?"

"But you never did say what that old lady wanted," Lisa pressed. "Did she want something? What did she say to you?"

"Not much. Nothing that made any sense, anyway," I said.

"Tell me," Lisa said. "Maybe I can help you figure out what she meant."

"What do you mean?" I set down the knife and stared at her. Did she know something I didn't know after all?

Lisa turned and looked in the direction of the back door. She was making sure Peggy and Dad weren't listening in. When she looked back, she seemed to be satisfied that they weren't. But she whispered anyway. "Jenna Reed told me this house is haunted."

"Haunted!" I thought of the outside of the house. I thought of the ugly living room curtains, and the wallpaper that looked like bread mold. Then I thought of the glowing blue light I thought I'd seen and the old woman's command to stay out of the tower. Could it be possible the house was actually haunted? It seemed almost silly, but...

"Shhh!" Lisa said, holding her finger to her lips. "My mom will be mad if she hears us talking about it."

"Well, who's Jenna Reed, anyway?" I asked.

"A girl I met the day I got here," said Lisa.

"How does she know about this house?"

"Jenna said all the kids around here know this house is haunted," Lisa said.

"Did she say anything about a blue light?" I asked.

"A blue light?" Lisa asked. Her eyes looked like two blue-green saucers. "What do you mean, a blue light? Did you see something?"

"Just a light," I said, trying to remember it. "It sort of...pulsed." I held up my hand and clenched and unclenched my fist to demonstrate. "Like that."

Lisa's arms were suddenly covered with goosebumps even though it wasn't cold. In fact, it was downright hot in that ancient kitchen. It was obvious that our talk about haunted houses and blue pulsing lights had scared her. It was beginning to scare me, too, and then all of a sudden, the screen door flew open. Both Lisa and I jumped.

"How's that salad coming?" Peggy asked. That's when Lisa fell off her stool. She must have bumped her head on the counter as she fell because the next thing I knew, Lisa was holding the side of her head and sobbing like a baby. Peggy rushed across the kitchen and gathered Lisa into her arms.

"There, there," Peggy crooned, rocking back and forth with Lisa. "It's all right, honey. Show me where you're hurt."

But instead of pointing to a spot on her head, Lisa wailed, "Diane saw it, Mom. I know she did."

"Saw what?" Peggy asked, looking over Lisa's blond head at me.

I shrugged. "I just told her I saw a light in the tower room window."

"A blue light that was moving!" Lisa said between sobs. "It was the ghost, Mom!" Lisa insisted. "Just like Jenna said. There's a ghost in this house, and Diane saw it!"

Peggy's lips tightened into a thin line. "I don't know what Diane thinks she saw, but this house is not haunted. It's merely old and a little run down," she said. "I've already told you that an old couple used to live here. I'm sure they kept to themselves, and they probably looked a little spooky to the kids in the neighborhood. But they most certainly weren't ghosts."

"Where are the burgers?" Dad asked, choosing that moment to come in through the back door. "The fire's hot." Then he looked at Peggy and Lisa, hugging each other on the yellowed linoleum. He frowned.

"Is everything all right?" he asked.

"The girls have been in here talking about ghosts, Ron," Peggy said. "They've worked themselves into a state over it, too. When I came in, Lisa was so jumpy, she fell right off the stool and hit her head on the counter."

"I haven't worked myself into a state," I insisted. But no one was listening to me, least of all Peggy.

"Have you been scaring Lisa, Diane?" Dad asked.

I shook my head. "I didn't bring up ghosts. Lisa did. All I said was that I saw a light in the tower room window while that old lady was here. The light sort of pulsed."

"That was the light from your skylight," Dad explained. He looked relieved that the answer to what I'd seen was so simple. "It probably 'pulsed,' as you put it, because of the clouds. You know—sun one minute, no sun the next."

"There," Peggy said firmly. "A simple and logical explanation. Now I want all talk of ghosts and haunted houses stopped. Do you girls understand?"

I nodded. Reluctantly, Lisa nodded, too.

Then Peggy stood up. She helped Lisa to

41

her feet. The two of them went to fix a bag of ice for Lisa to hold on her bruised head where a bump had sprouted. Dad made the hamburger patties himself and took them out to put on the grill. That left me to finish making the salad.

We ate outside at the picnic table in silence, except for a request now and then to have something like salad or ketchup passed. The tension in the air was so thick, I could feel it weighing down on me. Even though no one was bringing up the old woman or ghosts, I was pretty sure everyone was thinking about them. I know I was. I longed to get back to my little tower room where I could think whatever thoughts I wanted to think without being constantly watched. I'd been wrong to trust Lisa. I told myself I sure wouldn't do that again.

When dinner was finally over, Peggy, Lisa, and I cleaned up while Dad went into the basement to try to unclog the drain in the laundry tub. The silence continued until the last glass had been rinsed and put into the dishwasher. Then it was Lisa who spoke.

"Will you play a game with me, Diane?" Lisa asked. She seemed to have forgotten all about getting me in trouble over her friend's talk about ghosts. "I have a bunch of good board games we could play."

I shook my head. Playing a board game with Lisa was the last thing I wanted to do. "Not now," I said, trying not to sound as eager to get away from her as I felt, since I was sure I'd get into trouble for that, too. "I need to finish putting my stuff away."

"Later?" she wheedled.

I suddenly wanted to say, "Never!" But I didn't let myself. Instead, I said, "Not tonight. I'm really tired."

"Why don't you see if that little girl you met the other day wants to come over for a while, Lisa?" Peggy suggested.

"You mean Jenna?" Lisa asked.

Peggy nodded. "You could pop some popcorn and play one of your games with her right here at the kitchen table."

Lisa scowled. "I already told you, Mom. Jenna doesn't like this house."

"You could walk down there, then," Peggy went on pleasantly, pretending she didn't know that Lisa was talking about ghosts again.

But Lisa said, "I don't want to."

"I'm going up to my room," I said, edging toward the kitchen door. I didn't care what Lisa did, as long as it wasn't with me. Then, without saying any more, I hurried toward the stairs to the second floor. I took them two at a time because I couldn't wait to get away from the heavy atmosphere that seemed to cling to everything in the lower part of the house. I had a lot to think about...ghosts, haunted houses, and a crazy old lady. The only place I felt I could sort it out was in my little tower room.

But after I got to my bedroom, I paused before starting up the narrow staircase that would take me to the tower room. I couldn't shake off the old woman's warning:

"You must stay out of that room...be careful. You must be careful now, before it's too late."

I could almost hear the old woman's raspy voice again, and I felt a chill race along my skin.

But she'd been wrong, I told myself sternly. There was a logical explanation for the way the old woman acted, and there was a logical explanation for that blue light. I was making a big deal out of nothing. Worse, I was acting just like Lisa by letting myself get spooked.

I drew in a deep breath, and shook my head. The old woman was just confused. And the light was a trick of the clouds and the sun. That was all there was to it.

Five

I went up to my little room, ignoring the untouched suitcases I had to pass on the way. The last thing I wanted to think about was unpacking. Instead, I stretched out flat on the floor under the skylight. It was so peaceful up here, not at all the way that old woman had tried to make it sound.

I wasn't thinking about much of anything when all of a sudden, I had the distinct and uneasy feeling that I was no longer alone. I cocked my head and listened hard. Someone had gone into my bedroom below!

I got up and walked slowly to the stairs, then peered down through the open door. I didn't see anyone, but that didn't matter. I knew that someone was down there. I didn't have to see anyone. I could *feel* a presence. Then I heard a scuffling noise—the sound of sneakers on a bare wood floor. *Lisa*, I told myself. Then I heard a crash.

I dashed down the stairs. Lisa was bending over the broken fragments of the little china goose girl that Gran had given me.

"You broke it!" I shrieked, rushing over to Lisa and snatching the little white pieces away from her.

"I didn't," Lisa insisted. "It just fell off the shelf."

Her lower lip was trembling, and I could see tears welling up in her eyes. She was going to cry again. That was obviously Lisa's way of getting out of things. But I wasn't about to fall for her baby act the way Peggy did.

"Right," I said sarcastically, "after you touched it, it just fell off the shelf."

"But I *didn't* touch it," Lisa said.

"What are you doing in here anyway?" I demanded, stomping my foot. "I didn't say you could come in here. You didn't even knock first."

"But I was looking for you," Lisa insisted. Tears spilled out of her eyes and ran down her cheeks. "I wanted to talk to you about something. The door was open. I thought I heard you in here. Then when I stepped through the door, I saw the glass goose girl fall."

"You shouldn't have come in at all," I said.

I bent down and picked up the other pieces of the goose girl. There were so many, I knew it could never be fixed. I was so mad I wanted to throw all the fragments at Lisa.

"I'll knock next time," she promised weakly.

"Don't bother," I said. "I won't let you in. Not next time, not ever!"

Lisa must have known how angry I was because she started backing away from me. Tears continued running down her cheeks.

"What's going on in here?" Dad asked as he, too, stepped into my room without knocking or bothering to ask permission. "What's all the shouting about, Diane?"

"Look at this," I said, holding my broken goose girl out where he could see. "Lisa just came in here without knocking and broke this."

"I didn't," Lisa insisted. "It just fell off the shelf. I wasn't anywhere near it. It was like it jumped out at me or something."

"Right," I said sarcastically. "It jumped out at you. I suppose it's the figurine's fault it got broken."

"I didn't say it jumped," Lisa said with a sniffle. "I said it was *like* it jumped. You must have set it right on the edge of the shelf or something."

"Now *I'm* to blame?" I cried. "You come in here, uninvited, break my favorite glass piece and *I'm* to blame?"

"Maybe the ghost did it," Lisa suggested softly, looking at me and not Dad. I waited for Dad to call her on breaking her promise not to mention ghosts in the house. But, of course, he didn't.

"Now, girls," Dad said instead, coming further into the room. This was all Lisa's doing, but his tone made it sound like I was at fault, too. He held his hand toward me. "Give me the pieces, Diane. Maybe I can fix it."

But I closed my hand around the broken fragments, and tucked my hand behind my back, out of his reach. "You can't," I said. "Nobody can. It's smashed for good. But the worst part of it is that she's lying about it, Dad. Lisa broke it, and she won't even admit it. Aren't you going to punish her? At least tell her that she can never come in here again. Not ever!"

"We'll get you a new one, Diane," Dad said. "It's not that big of a deal. Really, it's not." He sounded impatient...with me!

"Maybe it's not a big deal to you, but it is to me! This was Gran's," I said. "She gave it to me, and that made it special." I shook my head angrily, then added, "I should have locked my door. From now on I will. It's the only way to get any privacy around here, I guess." I looked at Dad defiantly.

Now Dad was scowling, and I knew I'd gone too far. I could see that bringing up the locked door like that had only convinced him that I'd lied about locking it the first time. I considered taking my words back, but I knew it was already too late.

"Look, Diane," Dad began again, this time in an angry tone that was every bit a match for my own. But Peggy came in before he could demand that I give him the skeleton key, which is what I was sure he was about to do. Peggy took a quick look around, taking in the scene. It wasn't hard to guess that she wasn't going to be on my side, either.

"Oh, swell," I said, throwing myself backward onto my bed. "Why doesn't everyone come in. Break anything you want," I said sarcastically. "I don't have any rights, anyway. If I did have any rights, I wouldn't even be in this awful house to begin with. I'd be back in Springfield where I belong, with the people I love, the people who love me."

At that point, Peggy put her arm around Lisa and ushered her quickly and quietly out of the room. Dad and I were alone again. The sun was setting. My room was filled with eerie shadows. Dad continued to stand there, looking like he'd turned to stone.

"I'm disappointed in you, Diane," he finally said. "I thought we'd reached an agreement, but I guess I was wrong." His voice was cold. His face was almost impossible for me to make out in the darkness. But I could tell he was blaming me now for everything that had gone wrong that day...the old woman coming into the yard, Lisa's bump on the head, and finally my own broken glass figurine.

"You're going to have to make more of an effort to get along here," Dad said.

"Me!" I exclaimed. "What about Lisa?"

"We *all* need to make an effort," Dad continued. "But some of us are older and are expected to take on more of the responsibility for getting along *because* of being older. Being a family takes work, Diane. I knew this move, these changes, weren't going to be easy for you. But I never expected you to go out of your way to make things harder. This isn't like you."

"What do you know about me?" I demanded. "You don't even care what I want, not really."

"All right, then," Dad said. "What *do* you want?"

"I want to go back to Springfield and live with Gran like before," I said once again. "I want to go home."

"This is your home now, Diane," Dad said. "I don't know what kind of games you're playing here, but I want them to stop. You are not going back to Springfield so you may as well give up that idea once and for all. Nothing you do and nothing you say is going to change that." With that, Dad turned and left my room, pulling the door shut behind him.

I got off my bed and walked over to my desk. I opened the top drawer and took out the skeleton key. I locked the bedroom door, but I didn't leave the key in the lock. Instead, I took it up to my little tower room. There was a piece of string in my box of art supplies, and I threaded it through the top of the key. I was going to wear that key around my neck. I would never set it down. I would never part with it. I told myself I'd make them leave me alone. I'd make them stay out of my room.

Once the key was hanging safely around my neck, I lay beneath the skylight. I watched the sky turn darker and darker blue, telling myself that the old woman had definitely been wrong about this little room. There was nothing to be afraid of up here. It was only the light from the skylight that she'd seen and pointed out to me, just as Dad had said.

Maybe that's all that had ever really troubled that old woman about this house to begin with. Maybe she just didn't understand sky-lights and the way light comes through them. Maybe confusion about the light kept her coming back again and again. She was just trying to figure out what the funny light up in the tower was all about, and no one had bothered to explain.

Then it came to me, almost like a little voice had whispered it to me. I'd invite that old woman inside. I'd bring her right up to this room. I'd show her the skylight. She'd be satisfied once and for all then. She'd say, "Oh, I didn't know. Thank you." Then she'd go away and stop bothering Peggy.

After that, Peggy would relax. The kids in the neighborhood would stop talking about ghosts and start playing with Lisa. Lisa would discover that playing with other eight-year-olds was a lot more fun than playing with me. She'd leave me alone then. I'd have what I wanted and be a hero besides!

Then I heard a distant rumble. It was thunder. A summer storm was coming. I've always loved storms and looked forward to watching this one while lying beneath my very own skylight. I hurried downstairs to get the covers from my bed. *Tonight,* I thought happily, *I'll sleep up in my little tower room while the storm rages over and around me.*

I got back upstairs and settled beneath my covers just as the first flash of lightning streaked across the sky. Everything in my little room was illuminated for a moment, then vanished. I felt an icy wind sweep across the tower room.

Shivering, I sat up just as another bolt of lightning struck. In the moment of false daylight I thought I'd seen a girl sitting in the corner of the room. But in the next flash, I saw that I'd been wrong. There was no one there after all. But the image of that girl sitting there, looking so...terrified?...stayed with me anyway, and I began to feel uneasy.

Then there was another flash, and another. *There's no one here,* I told myself over and over again. *There's no one here but me.*

The thunder was growing louder now, and the flashes brighter and closer together. Then the rain started beating noisily against the skylight. I wanted to believe that no one, nothing, was with me. But somehow I couldn't. I didn't *see* anything anymore, but I still *felt* something there. And the feeling was like an icy hand on the back of my neck.

"I'm going back down," I said out loud as I stood up. I pulled my covers up with me. Then I paused, half expecting an answer. But, of course, no one said anything. The only sounds were of the storm as it swept by.

But now all the hairs on the back of my neck were standing up and goosebumps covered my arms and legs. My heart was racing, and I wanted to run down those narrow stairs. But I held back, afraid that if I ran, I'd be chased. I made myself walk down as casually as I could, and I forced myself not to look back.

When I was finally down the stairs, I dumped my blanket and sheets back on my bed. Then I walked quietly and cautiously over to my bedroom door and, taking the key from around my neck, unlocked the door again.

Now I was no longer locked in. But that wasn't quite enough. I was still uncomfortable. I opened the door just a sliver. The light from the hall seeped in, drawing a comforting line that went all the way to my bed, almost like an avenue of escape. That was better, but it still wasn't quite enough.

I walked back to the door of my little tower room and slowly shut it. Then, I looked down at the keyhole. It looked just like the keyhole in my bedroom door. Slowly, I lifted the skeleton key and slid it in. It fit, but would it work?

I began turning it. It turned easily, and finally, I heard the lock click into place. As it did, the wind let out a horrible shriek that sounded frighteningly like a person in pain.

Quickly, I walked back to my bed and straightened my covers out. *I didn't see anything up there,* I told myself firmly. I lay down, but I didn't go right to sleep. I couldn't. Somewhere in the house, someone was crying. *It must be Lisa*, I told myself. She was probably afraid of the storm. But, thinking of that girl huddled in the corner of my little room—or what I *thought* was a little girl—I wasn't at all sure I was right.

Six

"DIANE," I heard a faraway voice call. Opening my eyes just a little, I saw Gran. She was bending over me, smoothing my bangs from my forehead. I sighed contentedly, letting my eyes fall shut again. I felt warm and safe.

"Diane, honey. Wake up." I opened my eyes a second time, and saw that it wasn't Gran after all. It was Dad. I realized that I'd been dreaming.

"Hi," I said sleepily, still feeling dreamily pleasant from the illusion of waking up at Gran's.

Dad sat down on the edge of my bed and said, "I've got to go into the Edmonton office today." Dad is a salesman and he travels a lot. I blinked, trying to wake up, and saw then that he was dressed in a business suit. "I wanted to talk to you before I left, though."

I sat up. Then all the events of the day before quickly rolled through my mind again. I remembered the girl I thought I'd seen for just an instant. But I couldn't tell Dad about that. I knew it would only make him mad again. And anyway, I'd probably only imagined it. The storm was over. The sun was shining.

"I'm sorry for being so hard on you yesterday, Diane," Dad was saying. "None of the changes you're going through right now are easy. Regardless of what you may think, I *do* know that, honey. But I really do believe they're for the best or I wouldn't be asking you to make them." He gave me a small smile. "Anyway," he continued, "I woke you up to suggest that we wipe the slate clean and start fresh today. How about it, honey?" Dad tilted his head toward me hopefully.

I said, "I'll try."

"Good," Dad said cheerfully. "That's all I ask." He stood up. "Hurry and get dressed. We'll eat breakfast together."

As soon as Dad left, I got up and quickly got dressed. When I got to the kitchen, he was sitting at the table drinking coffee. Peggy was at the stove, cooking.

"I hope you like pancakes, Diane," Peggy said when she noticed me. While I watched, Peggy expertly flipped a perfectly browned pancake from the griddle to the warming plate.

"I don't just like them," I told her eagerly. "I love them! Those look like really good ones, too," I added.

"How about getting out the plates?" Peggy asked me.

"Sure," I said. "How many plates do we need?"

"Just three for now," Peggy said.

"Three? Where's Lisa? Isn't she on her way down?" Dad asked. "I thought you went to get her, Peg."

Peggy said, "I did. But she was still asleep. I decided to let her sleep a little longer. That storm kept her up half the night...and me, too," she added with a sigh.

I sighed then, too, but with relief. The crying I'd heard last night really had been Lisa after all.

"I think I'll go get her," Dad said. He stood up. "I'd like to eat breakfast with *all* of my family before going to work."

"Why don't you start eating, Diane?" Peggy flipped several pancakes onto a plate and handed it to me. "These are best right off the griddle."

I didn't argue. I was hungry and the pancakes smelled great. I carried the plate to the table where the butter and syrup were just waiting.

"Mmm," I murmured appreciatively after my first bite. "These are great."

Peggy smiled. "Thank you. It's an old family recipe. We'll make them together sometime. Okay?"

"Okay," I agreed. "I like to cook. I'm pretty good at it, too," I boasted. "I can make a chocolate cake from scratch." I sliced off another bite of pancake.

"About yesterday..." Peggy began.

"Maybe we should just forget about yesterday," I offered, and I meant it, too. I knew now that I'd been overtired. Today, everything seemed different.

"I'm not sure that's possible...or even a good idea, really," Peggy said. "You see, your father and I had a talk last night, Diane. Our talk made me realize that I haven't been giving you enough credit."

"What do you mean?" I asked.

"I guess I was thinking that you were younger than you really are. I realized I should have explained to you why having that old woman come around upsets me as much as it does. Lisa's only eight years old. Naturally, I didn't want to worry her. I wanted to protect her from even thinking about such things.

But, as your father pointed out, you're twelve. You'll be starting junior high soon. I can tell you things that Lisa is too young to understand."

But before Peggy could say anything more, Lisa came flying into the kitchen. She was wearing a white cotton nightgown. Her face was as deep red as the curtains in the living room. She had a baby doll clutched to her chest.

"Look!" Lisa commanded, thrusting the doll into her mother's face. I looked, too, and saw right away that only one sleeve of the doll's long-sleeved gown contained an arm.

Before either Peggy or I could say anything, Dad came into the kitchen. He was holding what I could tell at a glance was the doll's missing arm.

"Poor Amanda!" Peggy said of the doll. "What happened, honey?" I took another bite of my breakfast, only mildly interested in Lisa's reply.

But instead of answering her mother, Lisa spun on her heels and glared at me. Then everyone was glaring at me. It didn't take me long to figure out what they were thinking, either. They thought *I* was somehow responsible for Lisa's broken doll!

"Don't look at me," I said. "I didn't even

know you had that doll."

"You broke her on purpose," Lisa said, still glaring at me like I was a criminal.

"What do you know about this, Ron?" Peggy asked, turning to my father.

Dad shrugged. "Not much. I went into Lisa's room and called her. She sat up, then picked up that doll, which had been lying next to her. When she noticed the arm was missing, she started crying." He waved the doll's peach-colored arm at Peggy. "Then I found this a few feet away from Lisa's bed."

"You must have bumped her by accident in the night, honey," Peggy told Lisa gently.

Lisa shook her head violently. "No, Mom! That wouldn't pull Amanda's arm off." She pointed at me. "Diane did it because of that glass thing of hers. She's sure I broke it even though I said I didn't. Diane did it to get even with me. Diane hates me."

"I didn't touch your stupid doll," I said again. I was really getting steamed. Lisa had just ruined what had started out to be a nice morning. She'd also interrupted Peggy just when she was about to tell me more about the old woman. I couldn't help it. I said something I probably shouldn't have.

"Maybe that ghost of yours did it," I said sarcastically. Of course, I meant that maybe

Lisa herself broke the doll. But suddenly, the kitchen was in a state of havoc. Peggy exploded first.

"Diane!" Peggy gasped. "Please!"

"But you didn't hear her last night, Peggy!" I protested, trying to straighten out this new mess before it grew any bigger. "Last night before you came into my room, that's what Lisa was saying. According to Lisa, a ghost—and not Lisa herself—broke the china goose girl Gran gave me."

"Now girls," Dad said. He seemed to be including Peggy this time. "I'm sure I can fix the doll right up." He reached out as if to take Lisa's doll from her. But she pulled away from him. Melting into Peggy's side, Lisa burst into a fresh round of tears.

"I don't want her fixed," Lisa wailed. "I want her whole."

Peggy wrapped a protective arm around Lisa. "Amanda was Lisa's favorite doll," she explained to Dad with a weary sigh.

Then Dad turned to me as if he were going to say something. But instead of that, he wrinkled up his nose and frowned. "I smell smoke," he said. "Do you smell it, Peg?"

"Oh, no!" Peggy gasped. She raced to the griddle. "It's my pancakes!"

Just like the new start we were supposed

to be having that morning, the pancakes had gone up in smoke. With Lisa still clinging to her side, Peggy began scraping the burned pancakes off the scorched griddle.

With a groan, she said, "Now I'll have to scour the pan out before I make any more." Peggy nodded at the handful of pancakes still on the warming plate. "Here, Ron. You take these and start eating. Otherwise, you'll be late for your sales meeting."

"I don't really have time to eat now," Dad said, glancing at his wristwatch and then shaking his head.

"Of course, you do," Peggy insisted. Then she turned to Lisa and me. "Meanwhile, I want both you girls to go upstairs so Ron and I can have a moment to ourselves. We'll have to straighten this all out later."

"Fine!" Lisa said angrily. "I didn't want to get up in the first place." She glared at Dad. "He made me." Then she stormed out of the kitchen.

Peggy and Dad looked at me then. "I'm going," I told them before they could tell me to a second time. I got up and walked out of the kitchen. The swinging door that separated the kitchen from the dining room flapped shut behind me.

I'd only taken a step when I heard Dad say,

"It's going to be a lot harder than I thought, isn't it?"

I'd never been one to eavesdrop. But something made me stop. Peggy had said that she and Dad talked about me the night before. It seemed like they were about to have another discussion now. Since Peggy hadn't been able to tell me what conclusions they reached last night, I felt I almost deserved to hear what they were about to say now.

"I tried to do just what you suggested I do last night," I heard Peggy say. Her voice was slightly muffled, but I could hear all right. "Diane seemed to really like the way I was singling her out as an older girl, too. But then Lisa burst in before I could finish talking to her."

"Maybe that's just as well," Dad said with a sigh. "Maybe I was wrong about treating Diane more like an adult. Breaking Lisa's doll like that was a pretty childish thing to do."

I had to cover my mouth with my hand to keep from crying out. How could Dad even *think* I'd do something like that?

"So you think Diane broke Lisa's doll?" Peggy asked. She didn't sound surprised.

"Be honest, Peggy. Isn't that what you think?" Dad asked. I heard the sound of a fork scraping across a plate. Dad was eating the pancakes after all—and discussing me as if he were chatting about a weather report.

"I don't know what to think," Peggy said. "I wish I didn't have to think about any of it."

"It'll work out," Dad said soothingly. "You really didn't expect there to be no problems, did you?"

"I don't know what I expected, but I know I didn't expect this," Peggy said. "I don't know what I'm going to do when you leave town, Ron. I'm not sure I can manage if there's going to be a lot of yelling and destruction around here."

"I can't postpone my trip," Dad said. "I just can't."

"I know, I know," Peggy assured him. "But what should I do? I can't just let things go on like this, can I?"

"No. I think we have to do something positive. I have an idea that just might work, too," Dad said.

"Tell me," Peggy said.

"Well, Diane started baby-sitting a few months ago back in Springfield. From the reports I got, she did a very good job of it, too. Why not put Diane in charge next time you have to go out? Let her watch Lisa for you," Dad suggested.

"I don't know if that's such a good idea,"

Peggy said hesitantly. "What if she really did break Lisa's doll?"

"If she did do it, she had to have done it last night," Dad pointed out. "I really think she's ready to start over today."

"I thought so, too," Peggy agreed.

"Good," said Dad. "Then it's settled. I'm going to call them both down now and make them apologize to each other."

"Okay," Peggy said. But she still sounded like she didn't really want to trust me with her precious little brat. "I have to pick up my wallpaper order today. I shouldn't be gone very long. I'll leave Diane with Lisa then, and we'll see how it goes."

"Don't expect any overnight miracles to occur," Dad warned.

I heard a chair scrape against the floor, and I guessed Dad was standing up, getting ready to call us down. Peggy started to say something else, but I couldn't wait to hear what it was. I didn't want them to find out I'd been eavesdropping.

I backed slowly and carefully away from the door. Then, when I thought I was far enough away, I turned and ran up the stairs.

Seven

"I'M sorry your doll got broken," I told Lisa after we were all gathered in the kitchen again.

"And I'm sorry your glass goose girl got broken, too," Lisa said. We didn't sound like we meant it, and neither one of us had admitted anything. But Peggy and Dad seemed satisfied.

"There," Dad said. "Isn't that better?"

Peggy nodded, and Lisa and I both shrugged. We'd made a temporary truce. We'd been forced to. At the same time, we both knew no peace had been made.

"Well, I've got to go," Dad said. He picked up his briefcase. "I'll be home around six tonight." He gave us each a dutiful kiss and left.

"Do you want some more pancakes, Diane?" Peggy offered. "I'm going to make some more right now."

"No thanks," I said. "I'm going to go back up to my room."

"Still unpacking?" Peggy asked. I nodded, even though I still hadn't begun. "That's an awful job," she said. I nodded again. Then I hurried off.

Not only had I not started to unpack, I didn't intend to start unpacking now, either. I was going up to my little room to draw. Now that the sun was shining and the storm was all over, I felt silly for being afraid to be up there.

When I got up to my little tower room, I opened the window to let in some fresh air. This day promised to be even hotter than the day before, and it was already stuffy up in the small room.

Next, I took out a sheet of my best drawing paper and tacked it to an easel. Dad had made the easel for me the summer before when the two of us were still living with Gran.

I hummed a little as I got ready to work. This was a new day. I was still sad about the china goose girl getting broken. But at least that had taught me a valuable lesson. Lisa was never, *ever* going to come into my room again. I would try to act nice toward her to keep peace, but I was never going to trust her or let her near anything that was important to me. I decided that Lisa must have pulled the arm off her own doll. There was no other explanation. She probably did it so no one would think about how she had broken my knickknack, and to try to get me in trouble at the same time. As far as I was concerned, Lisa was worse than a brat. She was a monster.

I managed to do a fairly detailed sketch of Gran's house in Springfield and was just beginning to add watercolor paint when I heard voices in the yard. I walked to the window and looked out. Lisa and another girl were running around the unkept flower beds. Lisa was laughing and obviously having fun.

I guessed that the girl with Lisa was her new friend, Jenna Reed. Obviously, Jenna had gotten over her dread of the house just as Lisa had gotten over her broken doll.

I went back to painting Gran's house from memory, but was soon interrupted by a loud pounding on my bedroom door. My first reaction was to ignore it. I was sure it was Lisa and her friend. Lisa undoubtedly wanted to show her playmate my little room, but I had no intention of letting them in. The pounding didn't stop, though. It got louder and louder, and more and more insistent. With a sigh, I hurried down the stairs to tell the girls in person that they'd have to play someplace else. My room was off limits.

I flung open the door, all set to yell, "Go away!" But instead of Lisa and her friend, I found Peggy standing there.

"I have to go out for a few minutes," Peggy said. Her words sounded stiff and rehearsed. "I'm picking up some wallpaper samples I ordered. I was hoping you'd be willing to keep an eye on Lisa while I'm gone so I could leave her here. She's got her friend over."

"Okay," I said with a shrug. I was prepared for Peggy's request. I'd been rehearsing, too.

Peggy smiled. "Thank you so much, Diane." She was really going overboard now. "It's nice to have an *older* girl around I can count on. Lisa and her little friend Jenna are in Lisa's room playing a game. I should be back in about half an hour. They might not even come out until then."

"I've *baby*-sat before," I assured her, emphasizing the word "baby" to let her know just what I thought of Lisa. "I know what to do."

Peggy opened her mouth as if to say something else, but then all she said was good-bye. She hurried downstairs. I heard the front door open and shut. Then I heard her small, compact car start and zoom away.

I could hear Lisa and Jenna laughing in Lisa's room. Even though I wanted to keep working on my painting, I didn't think I should until Peggy got back.

So, instead, I wandered downstairs. It was too early for lunch, but I still felt a little hungry. I never did get to finish my pancakes this morning, I reminded myself. I went into the kitchen to look for something to eat. I found an apple in a bowl on the counter and took it into the living room.

I took a big bite of my apple and wandered over to the front window. Pulling aside those awful, blood-red curtains, I peered outside.

The yard in front of the house was just as dark as it had been the day before, even though the bright summer sun was beating down everywhere else. I looked up at the scraggly trees that were supposed to be causing all this shade and shook my head. It didn't seem possible. There just weren't that many leaves up near the top of either one of them. Something else had to be keeping the sun out. Then, shivering slightly, I thought of the girl I thought I'd seen up in my little room. Slowly, I let my eyes travel down the trunk of the nearest tree.

That's when I spotted the old woman coming through the overgrown hedge along the driveway. She stopped in front of the hedge and looked directly at the front window where

I was standing. Quickly, I let the curtains drop. My heart was pounding and I could hardly breathe. I didn't know what I was frightened of, though. I'd already talked to her and she had seemed harmless enough.

I decided it was her warning. "Stay out of that tower room!" she'd said. But I hadn't. Was that why she was back?

I sat down on the couch and stared at the single bite I'd taken out of my apple. What should I do? Go out and tell her to go away? Stay put and hope that she'd just go away on her own? Or should I invite her in to show her the skylight? That had seemed like a good idea the night before. On the other hand, what would Lisa say if she saw the old woman again? I didn't know, and I didn't want to find out. Peggy left me in charge and I wanted to show her that I could be trusted.

I was still trying to decide what to do when the doorbell rang. I jumped a mile. I'd never expected the old woman to be that bold. But then, what did I really know about her?

The doorbell rang again, and I wondered if I should call the police. After all, that was what Dad said he'd do if the old woman came back again.

But I wasn't sure what I'd say to the police. After all, the old woman hadn't really done anything wrong. She hadn't even threatened me. I didn't think a person could be arrested for *warning* another person, but I didn't know.

I was still trying to decide what to do when I heard giggling and the thunder of four sneakered feet pounding down the stairs.

"Who's at the door?" Lisa demanded when she saw me. "Aren't you going to answer it? Where's Mom?"

"Your mother went out for a little bit, and, no, I'm not going to answer the door," I said, having just decided.

"Why not?" Lisa's friend asked. She'd been smiling, but now she wasn't.

"Are you Jenna?" I asked. She had reddish-brown curls. They jiggled like gelatin when she nodded yes. Then, before I could stop her, Lisa hurried over to the window.

"Lisa!" I cried, grabbing for her. But Lisa dodged my grasp and yanked aside the curtains.

"It's a girl," Lisa announced. This time, whoever it was knocked, probably deciding the doorbell didn't work.

"Let me see," Jenna said as she joined Lisa at the window. "Oh," Jenna said with a giggle. "It's my sister, Stacey!"

"Open the door, Diane," Lisa insisted. "Let

Jenna's sister in."

"Maybe she won't even want to come in," Jenna said. She made her eyes round. Then she lifted her hands in a way that was supposed to be scary and said, "Whooooo!"

Lisa pretended to look frightened. "A ghost!" she cried. "Oh, no! Save me, Diane!" She covered her mouth with her hands and pretended to quiver.

"Knock it off, you two," I told them, annoyed. "There's no ghost stuff allowed around here, and you know it, Lisa." I could just imagine what Peggy would say if she heard them carrying on about ghosts. I knew who'd get in trouble for it, too. Me.

I stalked to the front door and pulled it open. It was the girl I'd seen at the door the day before.

"Hi," she said pleasantly. "I'm Stacey Reed. I live down the street."

"Hi. I'm Diane," I told her.

"Is my sister, Jenna, here?" she asked. "My mom wants her to come home."

"She's right here." I turned around, but Lisa and Jenna were gone. "Well, she was right here. I guess she and Lisa ran off somewhere. Come on in. We'll hunt them down together."

I stepped aside to make room for Stacey to come in. At the same time, I looked over her shoulder to see if the old woman was still out in the yard. Thankfully, she'd gone.

As I shut the front door again, I heard the two younger girls go pounding up the stairs, giggling all the way. A door on the second floor slammed.

Stacey looked at me and rolled her eyes. "Aren't little sisters a pain?"

I shrugged. "Actually, Lisa isn't really my sister. Her mom is just married to my dad."

"You're stepsisters, then," Stacey said. "Little stepsisters are probably just as bad as little sisters."

"Probably worse," I said. We both laughed.

Then she looked at the apple I was holding. "Got another one of those?" she asked. "I'm starved."

"Sure," I said. I led the way to the kitchen. Now that I had someone my own age to talk to, everything seemed a little more normal.

"Jenna's in trouble, as usual," Stacey told me as she picked an apple from the bowl on the counter. "She wasn't supposed to take off this morning until she'd cleaned her room. She told Mom she had, but when Mom looked in there a little bit ago, I guess it was still a mess. Anyway, I'm in no rush to bring her back."

"Good. Want to sit down for a minute, then?" I asked Stacey, leading her toward the kitchen table.

Stacey nodded. "Sure." She pulled out a chair. "I'm going into seventh grade next year. How about you?"

"Me, too," I said. "What's the junior high like in Edmonton?"

Stacey grinned. "Great! I can't wait. Sixth grade was a bore." She rolled her eyes again. "Anyway, I'm glad I'll be riding a different bus and going to a different school than Jenna. She can be such a tattletale."

"I know what you mean," I agreed. We both ate some more of our apples. "By the way, did you see anyone in the yard when you came up?" I asked.

Stacey nodded. "Cassandra Day was out there when I walked up." Stacey shook her head and rolled her eyes again. "She took off when I said hello to her, though. Boy, is she weird."

"Cassandra Day," I said, repeating the name.

Stacey nodded again. "She's as crazy as a loon, according to my dad."

"My dad says the same thing," I told Stacey. "But what does that really mean?" I asked.

"It means she walks around talking to herself, for one thing," said Stacey. "Most people try to stay away from her. That isn't exactly hard to do, either. If anyone says anything to her, especially a kid, she usually hurries away like she did just now when I said hi." Stacey paused to swallow a bite of apple. "My mom says Cassandra Day is disturbed. But I guess she isn't dangerous, or they'd lock her up. I've seen her around all my life, but she still gives me the creeps. No one likes her. She doesn't have a single friend."

"That's kind of sad," I said.

Stacey shrugged. "I guess," she said.

"Anyway, she didn't run away from me yesterday," I told Stacey. "Yesterday, she came right up to me when I was outside in the backyard, and she started talking to me. She told me I should stay out of the tower room."

"She has got a thing about this house," Stacey said, taking another bite of her apple and looking around the kitchen. "The thing is," she continued, pausing for a second to swallow, "Cassandra Day used to live here."

Eight

"HERE?" I asked. "That old woman lived here?"

Stacey nodded. "Didn't you know?"

"No," I said, stunned. "I had no idea." I was pretty sure Peggy and Dad must have known, though. I figured that was probably what Peggy had been about to tell me earlier when Lisa burst into the kitchen with her broken doll.

"I didn't always know," Stacey admitted. "I just found out about it at the beginning of summer when Mom told us. The kids around here had decided your house was haunted when Cassandra Day started hanging around it all the time. She'd stare up at the second floor, pointing and talking to herself. Anyway, Mom thought if we knew we'd understand."

"Knew what?" I asked.

Stacey shrugged. "That she lived here once.

We already knew she was more than a little crazy. Mom said that Cassandra was probably seeing ghosts...but they were ghosts only she could see, ghosts from her past. Mom said a lot of people get like that, especially when they get older. It's part of memory, she says."

"But why did she just start coming around now? Why didn't she bother the old couple who used to live here?" I asked Stacey. "They were here just before Peggy and Dad bought the house, right?"

Stacey nodded. "That's right. Their name was Biddle. I don't know why Cassandra never bothered them. Maybe she was afraid of them or something."

"When exactly did Cassandra Day live here?" I asked. "Do you know?"

Stacey nodded. "It was a long time ago, when she was just a little girl, according to my mom."

"How does your mom know so much about it?" I wondered.

"Local history is Mom's hobby," Stacey explained. "She does volunteer work at the Edmonton Historical Society a couple of times a week. She also writes articles on historical landmarks and other things like that for the *Edmonton Sentinel*."

"Maybe something happened to that old

lady here, and she keeps coming back to think it over," I suggested.

"That's what my mom was saying, all right," Stacey agreed.

"Do you think something Dad or Peggy said set her memory off or something?"

"It's possible, I guess," Stacey said.

"I wonder what it could have been?" I said.

"Anything really," Stacey replied. "Like I told you, Cassandra Day is crazy." Then Stacey looked at me thoughtfully. "Do *you* think this house is haunted, Diane? Have you seen anything yourself...besides 'Old Lady Day' hanging around?"

I looked at Stacey for a moment, debating whether or not to tell her what I thought I had seen. I finally decided to tell her about the flickering blue light and see how she took that. If she didn't make fun of me, I would tell her about the girl huddled in the corner of my little room—or at least what I thought had been a girl. But just then, Jenna and Lisa came bouncing into the kitchen.

"I came to bring you home, you know," Stacey told Jenna.

"Why?" Jenna asked.

"Because you didn't finish cleaning your room like you promised Mom you would," Stacey explained.

Jenna sighed. "Tell Mom I did the best I could," she said.

Stacey shook her head. "You tell her that yourself. We better go, Jenna," Stacey said, "before Mom gets any madder at you than she already is."

"Not yet," Jenna pleaded. She scooped an apple out of the bowl Lisa held out to her.

"Well, okay," Stacey said, sitting back down. "Just a few more minutes, though, and then that's it. No complaining, either."

"I promise," Jenna said.

Meanwhile, I saw that Lisa was handling every apple in the bowl, making a big show of it. Finally she found one that suited her. Plucking it out, she took a noisy bite. I fumed a little. She was just trying to bug me.

"Let's take these out back, Jenna," Lisa said. Jenna nodded, and they ran out through the back door, giggling.

As soon as they were gone, Stacey asked, "Where were we before we were so rudely interrupted?"

"We were talking about Cassandra Day," I reminded her.

"That's right," Stacey said. "So—is or isn't this house haunted?"

"My dad claims it isn't," I said, having decided to hold my opinion back a little longer. "Lisa's mom won't talk about it. She doesn't want us to talk about it, either. I guess Lisa gets too scared. Anyway, Dad's a little calmer about it, but he definitely backs Peggy up. Yesterday, they were talking about calling the police the next time Cassandra Day shows up. They're really fed up with her, I guess."

"Maybe," said Stacey. "Or maybe they're afraid Cassandra Day is right about this house. Maybe they think this house is haunted, too."

"You might be right," I said thoughtfully. It did seem like Dad had been just a little too quick to explain away the blue light. *Had he seen it himself?* I wondered. And what about the girl I'd thought I'd seen in the corner of the tower room? Maybe that had been a ghost!

"You *have* seen something, haven't you, Diane?" Stacey leaned across the table and waved her half-eaten apple at me. "Are you going to tell me about it, or not? Because, if you are, I'll wait. If you're not, I better get Jenna home. My mother is probably furious by now."

"Want to see my room before you go?" I asked quickly, trying to change the subject. I wasn't ready to tell Stacey, I decided. What

I knew was too vague and wild. I still thought I might have imagined everything. After all, the day before hadn't been an easy one. I'd been tired and upset about the move. But I still didn't want Stacey to go.

"Is that where the ghost is?" Stacey asked. She looked a little nervous.

I cleared my throat and stood up, trying to figure out what to say.

"It *has* been there, right?" Stacey asked triumphantly. "I can tell by your face!"

I realized I'd given away too much, even without saying anything specific. But there was no turning back now. If I wanted Stacey for a friend, I knew I should be honest with her. But, if I was honest, she might decide I was as crazy as old Cassandra.

"I'm not sure," I said vaguely. And that was the truth. "Anyway, if I *did* see a ghost, it was a fleeting sort of thing. I'd have to see it again to be really sure."

Stacey said, "Okay, then. Let's take a look. But it'll have to be a quick one."

I led the way out of the kitchen and across the dining room. We reached the stairs to the second floor. I stopped and Stacey stopped, too, waiting for me to go up first.

"My room is at the end of the hall," I said. I started up the stairs. Stacey was following

83

so close behind me now that I could hear her breathing. She was so nervous, it was making me nervous.

"It's really big, isn't it?" was the first thing Stacey said once we were actually in my room.

"It's at least twice as big as my old room at my grandmother's house," I answered. "Anyway, eventually I'm going to get curtains and a bedspread to match. I've decided on the color already, too. Lilac. The room will seem friendlier then." I noticed that Stacey was looking at me funny.

"What's wrong?" I asked her.

"How can you sleep in here if you actually think this room is haunted?" she asked. "Aren't you scared?"

As soon as she asked, I realized I wasn't. "If there is a ghost," I explained, "it's only a girl, like us. I think she's lonely. She seems to be afraid of storms, too," I added, realizing as I did that I no longer doubted what I'd seen last night. I went on, "I saw her. It was only for a moment. But I'm sure now, after talking to you, that she was really there."

"Really where?" Stacey asked.

"Upstairs." I pointed at the door to my little room. "In the tower room. But only for a second. It happened last night, during that storm. Want to go up?" I asked.

Stacey looked at the closed door and shuddered. She hesitated a moment, but finally said, "Sure, why not? Ghosts don't come out in the day, anyway...do they?"

I thought of the pulsing blue light Cassandra Day had pointed out to me the afternoon before. But I didn't mention that to Stacey. Instead, I said, "I don't really know very much about ghosts, to tell you the truth. This is my first experience with one."

Stacey giggled nervously. "Me, too." But I noticed that once again she waited for me to lead.

As soon as I opened the door to the tower room, light flooded down the stairs. A blast of cold air came sailing down the stairs with it. I shivered. Stacey did, too.

"That's quite a draft," she commented. "Isn't it usually hot the higher up in a house you go?"

I nodded. "Usually," was all I said. And after all, earlier in the day it *had* been hot. Still, it seemed obvious by now that my little room was pretty unusual.

"It's so light up there," Stacey said as we slowly neared the top of the narrow staircase. "I never expected it to be so light." She sounded relieved.

"It's from a skylight," I explained. "My dad

knows I like to draw and paint, so he had the skylight put in for me so I could have my own art studio."

We'd crossed the room in a couple of steps and were now standing directly under the skylight.

"Oooh!" Stacey exclaimed, looking up. "Look at the clouds roll by!"

"Well," I said after we'd stood for a while watching them, "What do you think? Is it haunted or not?"

Stacey looked around the little room. There was nothing up there but my box of art supplies and my easel. "It's so empty. I mean, there's no place to hide, is there?" she asked.

"I don't think ghosts need to hide, Stacey. I think they just disappear when they don't want to be seen anymore."

"Oh," she said quietly. Her eyes darted around the room another time.

"Cassandra Day told me to stay out of this room yesterday," I confided to Stacey.

"You mean, she threatened you?" Stacey asked.

I shook my head. "I don't think it was a threat. It was more of a...warning."

Suddenly, someone outside screamed. Stacey and I raced to the window to look out. I was half expecting to see Cassandra Day down there, possibly hassling Lisa like she'd hassled me the day before. But there was no Cassandra.

Instead, I saw Jenna, sitting on the ground crying. Lisa was standing over her. She had her hands on her hips. From where Stacey and I stood, it was impossible to tell what had happened.

"We better go check it out," Stacey said, already hurrying toward the stairs.

Nine

"WHAT happened?" Stacey asked her little sister once we were outside.

"She pushed me," Jenna said. She pointed an angry finger at Lisa. Lisa looked angry, too. She had that same pinched look she'd had after breaking my china goose girl. She had also looked like that after accusing me of breaking her doll.

"Lisa," I said, feeling my own anger at her flooding to the surface, "how could you?

"I didn't mean to run into Jenna," Lisa sputtered. Her lower lip began to quiver as a giant tear spilled out of her eye and slid down her cheek. "We were playing tag and I tripped. That's all." She pointed at Jenna. "She thinks I pushed her on purpose. But I didn't."

"Really?" Jenna asked. She had stopped crying and sounded eager to forgive Lisa.

Lisa looked down at her and nodded bashfully. "Really. It was an accident. I'm sorry, Jenna." Jenna might have been ready to let the whole thing drop, but I wasn't. I couldn't allow Lisa to keep getting away with her lies. They'd only get bigger if I did.

"You're a real jerk, Lisa!" I said. "You think you can just get out of the awful things you do by crying."

"Hey!" Stacey said, putting her hand on my shoulder. "Aren't you being a little hard on her, Diane? Jenna's all right. I mean, this kind of stuff happens when kids play."

But I was too angry about everything to admit to anyone—especially Lisa—that I'd gotten carried away. Instead, I turned away. That's when I noticed the strange blue glow up in the tower room window.

More fascinated than frightened, I stood there watching the glow slowly take the form of a girl! It was the same girl I'd seen crouched in the corner of the tower room during the storm. But it wasn't just a girl. I knew then I was looking at a ghost! It had to be. And the ghost was gazing down at us.

Then I heard someone groan. Turning sharply, I found myself face to face with Cassandra Day. She, too, was looking up at the tower room window. She lifted her finger and pointed at the ghost. Her face was as pale and gray as fog, and her old mouth was hanging open.

I looked back up at the window just in time to see the ghost lift her finger and point back. I heard Cassandra gasp and groan again.

"Her power is growing," Cassandra said softly. "We'll never stop her now."

"Who is she?" I asked. "I know you know. Tell me!"

At the sound of my voice, Cassandra pulled her eyes away from the ghostly figure in the window and focused them on me.

"You!" she said accusingly. "The two of you are just alike. That's the trouble. She's been waiting for someone like you. I knew she was waiting. But I'd hoped she'd have to wait forever. She wants revenge now, and she knows that you'll help her get it."

With each word Cassandra uttered, I felt myself shrinking. I wanted to scream that I was innocent. But the way Cassandra looked at me filled me with guilt. Was Cassandra right? Was I somehow to blame for the appearance of this ghost? Had I unknowingly called her forth? Or was Cassandra just trying to pin her own guilt on me?

Meanwhile, Stacey, who'd dropped down on the ground next to Jenna, was scrambling to her feet. "Go away!" she ordered Cassandra.

"Go away, right now. Go home where you belong and leave us alone, you crazy old lady!"

"You can't see her now, can you?" Cassandra whispered to me in a raspy voice, ignoring Stacey's outburst.

I glanced up at the window. The ghost was gone. There wasn't even a flicker of the blue light.

"But she's still there," Cassandra said, her eyes narrowing. "I can *feel* her there. She's waiting, and she won't go now until she gets what she's come for."

"What *has* she come for?" I cried. "If you know, you have to tell me! Who is she?"

I was still waiting for Cassandra to answer when I heard Peggy's car pull into the driveway. Before Peggy had even turned off the engine, Cassandra was hurrying across the lawn. She slipped back through the hedge and was gone.

"I'm telling Mom that spooky old lady was here again," Lisa said. But she wasn't moving. She was just standing, rooted to the spot where she'd been when Cassandra arrived. Lisa was actually trembling. *Had she seen the ghost in the tower room window?* I wondered. But she couldn't have. Surely if Lisa had seen anything, she'd have said so. Jenna, too. But what about Stacey?

91

"No," I said. "Don't tell your mom, Lisa. Please don't. She'll just get upset. You know she will. There's nothing she can do about it now, anyway."

"I don't think any of us should mention Old Lady Day's visit," Stacey said.

Lisa and Jenna exchanged looks.

"Really," Stacey insisted. "Our mother would probably get upset just like Lisa's mother, Jenna. Cassandra didn't really do anything to any of us. She just said a lot of dumb stuff. Right? If our mothers get upset, they might decide not to let us play together...at least for awhile. You know how mothers are."

"Stacey's right, you know," I said.

"Okay," Lisa and Jenna agreed.

"Well, we'd better go home now, Jenna," Stacey said, helping her sister to her feet. "Mom will be wondering where we are, and she's already mad at you for not finishing your room."

Jenna nodded, then turned to Lisa. "Come with me, Lisa," she said. "My mom won't stay mad at me if you're with me."

"Okay," Lisa said.

With that, the two of them took off.

"I'd better go with them," Stacey said. She turned to go. "Were you kidding me up there,

Diane? Or is there really a ghost?"

"Didn't you see her?" I asked, now that the little girls were gone.

"You mean Cassandra?" Stacey asked, drawing her eyebrows together in a question.

"No," I said impatiently. "The ghost. It was up in the tower room window. Cassandra saw it just now. I saw it, too. It pointed at Cassandra. Didn't you see how scared she was?"

"The ghost?" she asked, slowly backing away from me.

"No," I said. "Not the ghost. Cassandra." Then I shook my head. How had Stacey missed it? Had she just not looked up? Or was the ghost only visible to Cassandra and me? Somehow, I found this last thought the most frightening of all. *Why me,* I wondered? The ghost must want something from me, but what? So far, it had been harmless, even nice. But what if I didn't do what Cassandra seemed to think the ghost wanted me to do? What then? It was obvious Stacey didn't know what to think of me at this point.

Somehow, I managed to turn a shudder into a laugh. "Pretty funny, huh?"

Stacey's eyes narrowed. "Oh, you! I was beginning to believe you, too."

"You didn't think I really believed in ghosts, did you?" I asked. I'd decided I didn't want my new friend to think I was as crazy as Cassandra. I needed a friend my own age. If I couldn't be friends with Stacey, I'd have no one but Cassandra Day and the ghost to talk to. There seemed to be something going on between Cassandra and the ghost, and I seemed to be caught in the middle of it.

"Why don't you come over later?" Stacey said, still backing slowly away from me. "We live three doors down. Come over after lunch." Then Stacey turned and ran after Lisa and Jenna.

Once I was alone, I looked back up at the window to my little room. It looked like all the other windows at the back of the house now. Cassandra and I had both seen a ghost up there just a few minutes ago. I was sure of it. Even though I'd denied it to Stacey, I now knew for sure that the house on Dorsey Avenue was haunted.

I reached up and touched the skeleton key that was hanging around my neck. *Useless,* I told myself. Locked doors wouldn't keep a ghost out or in. Even I knew that. Who was she, anyway? Why she was there? And, most importantly, what did she want from me?

It seemed that the only way I was going to learn the answers to my questions was by asking either Cassandra or the ghost herself.

I was sure I wasn't going to find out what I wanted to know until they were ready to tell me.

Even though the hot August sun was beating down on me now, I shivered. There was no one I could confide in. No one would even believe it if I told them. I'd never felt so alone in my life.

*   *   *   *   *

Dad left on a sales trip the next morning. Peggy, of course, didn't want him to leave. But I was used to the time Dad spent traveling. He wouldn't have been able to help me sort out this thing with Cassandra and the ghost, anyway. In fact, having Dad gone was almost a relief. It meant one less disbeliever in the house for me to worry about.

During the next few days, I spent as much time in the yard as I spent in the house. I was waiting for either Cassandra or the ghost or both of them to come back to me at the same time. When they did, I planned to demand answers. But as the days passed, neither one appeared. If they were around, they kept out of my sight. I was almost able to put the whole mess out of my mind—almost.

Stacey and I were getting to know each

other better. We talked about our favorite rock groups, and we talked about boys. But we didn't talk about Cassandra Day or the tower room ghost. I knew I'd spooked Stacey at first by telling her I did believe there was a ghost. And then I confused her by acting like I'd just been joking. I was afraid that if I brought it up again, she wouldn't know how to take me. But not mentioning those things left a wedge between us. We were friends, but we weren't best friends.

I kept my skeleton key around my neck and used it all the time. I still didn't trust Lisa, or even like her very much. But I was resigned to doing what I could to make the best of my situation. Lisa didn't like my locked door, of course. But I didn't care. I treated her like she didn't exist and she kept her distance. Nothing more of mine or hers got broken, either.

Thankfully, Lisa had Jenna to play with, and that took her out of the house a lot. I was able to draw and paint up in my little room without interruption while waiting for the ghost to come back.

One afternoon I was over at Stacey's house. We were sitting on the Reeds' front porch, talking about Edmonton Junior High School where we would both be going in September.

As usual, Lisa and Jenna came up to us.

"I want to go home and show Jenna your tower room. Can I?" Lisa asked me. She made it sound like it was no big deal. But, of course, we both knew better. I'd told her I didn't want her in my little room, no matter what. I didn't even let her up there when I was there...especially not when I was there.

"No," I snapped, my hand going instantly to the key that was hanging where it always hung—around my neck. "Stay out of my room."

"See," Lisa said to Jenna. "I told you she was too mean to say yes. But one day, when she goes, it'll be my room. My mom promised me. Then we'll go up there."

"What do you want to do up there, anyway?" Stacey asked the girls.

Jenna shrugged, but Lisa said, "I just want to show Jenna. It's the best room in the house and Diane keeps hoarding it."

"When it's yours," I said, "you can go in all you want. While it's still mine, you can't." I couldn't explain that the real reason I didn't want them up there was because they might stir up the ghost.

"Come on, Jenna," Lisa said. "We'll do something else at my house. I don't want to go into Diane's stinky, old room, anyway." Jenna nodded, and they both stormed off.

"Aren't you kind of hard on Lisa?" Stacey asked.

"I suppose you think I should just let her play in that room," I said defensively.

"No," said Stacey. "I don't let Jenna go in my room, either, not unless I'm there. But you could have been nicer about saying no. It might be easier on both of you if you got along better."

I shook my head. "You don't know Lisa. She lies. She's a sneak, too. It's impossible to trust her."

"Maybe if you were nicer to her, she'd stop being so awful," Stacey volunteered.

"You're beginning to sound like Peggy," I told her. I didn't mean that as a compliment, and I could tell that Stacey knew it.

We looked away from each other. I stood up and cleared my throat. Already, I felt rotten for saying that. "Well, I'd better get on home," I told Stacey. "No telling what Lisa and Jenna will get into if I don't keep an eye out for them."

She looked as if she were about to say something, but I added a quick, "See you later," then hurried back to the house as quickly as I could.

Ten

"**D**IANE?" I heard Peggy call to me as I came in the back door. "Is that you?"

"Yes," I called back. "It's me."

"Come in here, please." Peggy had started stripping wallpaper off the living room walls the day Dad left. Though she'd worked on it constantly since then, she still wasn't finished. She'd discovered three more layers of wallpaper under the one that showed, and she claimed each layer was harder to get off than the first. But Peggy had a goal. She was determined to have the new paper up when Dad got back from his sales trip. Now she had less than a week to go.

As I walked toward the living room, I was afraid she was going to ask me to help her peel wallpaper. I'd done a little of that already, and it was a horrible job. I walked slowly, trying to come up with a good excuse, one that would get me out of it without sounding too flimsy.

"Peggy?" I said, squinting into the dim room.

"We need to talk, Diane," Peggy said. Her voice was low and she spoke slowly. I saw the stepladder she usually stood on to work, but she wasn't on it. Finally, I saw her sitting on the couch. Then I saw a hand mirror with a fancy silver handle lying across her lap. The face of the mirror was smashed into cracks so fine it looked like a spider web.

I continued looking down at the mirror. Even with all those cracks, it was catching light from somewhere in the dark room.

"What happened to that?" I asked, stopping in the archway that separated the living room from the dining room.

"I think you should tell me," Peggy said.

I shrugged. "I don't know. I've never seen it before. Is it yours?"

"You know very well that it's mine, and I think you've seen it before," Peggy said. Her voice was stiff and cool. She sounded very angry.

"You're blaming me, aren't you?" I asked. "But you're wrong. I didn't break your mirror. I really have never seen it before."

"Don't lie, Diane. It won't do any good. I

know what you're up to. You meant to make some kind of twisted point by doing this, didn't you? Somehow you knew this mirror belonged to my grandmother. It is one of the few things I had to remind me of her and all that she meant to me. That's why you broke it, isn't it?"

I gasped. "But that's so unfair!" I exclaimed. "I'm not lying. I'm not. You must think I'm some kind of a monster. But I'm not. You better ask Lisa what she knows about this if you want to know the truth."

"Don't try blaming Lisa again," Peggy warned. "This mirror meant as much to her as it did to me. And anyway, I already showed it to her and knew without even asking her that she didn't do it. I could tell by the look on her face. Lisa was just as upset by this deliberate act of vandalism as I am. As I'm sure your father will be."

I could just imagine Dad's face. He'd take their side, and all because I'd told him I wanted to stay in Springfield instead of moving to Edmonton. *It didn't pay to be honest,* I told myself. In this house liars came out ahead.

Peggy shook her head. "I thought we'd all been getting along so well since your dad left, Diane. I thought the worst was behind us. I even thought we were beginning to be friends."

"Friends! You never believe me!" I shouted. "I didn't break your mirror, but that doesn't matter to you, does it? It's broken and your precious Lisa couldn't have done anything that awful, so it must be me, right? Well, as usual, you're wrong. It wasn't me!"

"I think you'd better go up to your room, young lady. You have a lot to think about," Peggy said. I could tell she was doing all she could to control her own fury.

"Fine," I said. "There isn't anywhere else in this stupid house I'd rather be, anyway."

"You'll stay up there until you're ready to apologize," Peggy added.

"I'll just stay up there forever, then. I'm never going to apologize for something I didn't do!" I turned and stormed up the stairs to the second floor. As I passed Lisa's room, I glanced in and saw Lisa and Jenna sitting on the floor. They were playing a board game, and didn't look up. But they probably heard every word Peggy had said. It made me even angrier.

When I got to the door to my bedroom, I stopped and pulled out the skeleton key. The door was still locked, just the way I'd left it before going over to Stacey's. I unlocked it, hurried in, then slammed the door as hard as I could.

Still angry and hurt, I climbed the stairs to my little tower room. I'd started a new watercolor of Gran's house earlier that morning. I'd gone over to Stacey's on a kind of break. Even though I was angry at being unfairly accused and punished, I was eager to get back to my art. This painting looked like it would turn out to be the best thing I'd ever done, and I planned on sending it to Gran as a present.

But as soon as I reached the top stair, I saw that my beautiful painting was ruined. Someone had painted a big, red "X" right through the picture! A wide paint brush I rarely used was lying on the wooden floor next to the easel. The brush was in a pool of red paint.

First I gasped, then I sank to the floor. This was the worst thing Lisa had done so far, I decided. It was worse than mean. It was vicious. I wanted to strangle Lisa, that's how angry I was. She had no right.

Then I remembered the key! The door to my bedroom had been locked, and I had the only key. Whoever—or whatever—had ruined my picture had been *in* the room when I locked the door. Then I shook my head. But that was impossible, too! Or was it?

Slowly I turned around in a full circle, carefully examining every inch of my little room. I saw nothing but my art supplies, my easel, my ruined painting, that horrid paint brush, and the puddle of red paint.

Then, all at once, I stomped my foot. "What do you want from me?" I cried out angrily. I crumpled up my picture and tossed it into the wastebasket.

"Well?" I demanded, turning in a circle again. I was more than angry. I was furious. "I'm waiting for an answer!"

All at once, I felt a blast of icy air sweep over me. I had the eerie feeling that someone was in the room with me now. I'd had the same feeling in the little room before. But this time the feeling was so strong that I actually took a step back.

I whispered, "What do you want? Tell me! Please, tell me!"

I still couldn't see anyone, but a voice inside my own mind seemed to direct me to the window. I went over and looked out.

There was Cassandra Day, and I wasn't at all surprised. At first, I thought she was looking at me. But I quickly realized that she was looking *past* me. Even from that distance, I could see that her eyes were filled with dread. Slowly, she raised her gnarled finger and pointed. Her mouth dropped open like she intended to shout something, or maybe even scream. But no sound came out. It was as if she were frozen.

Slowly, as if in a dream, I turned around. What I saw made my heart pound.

The ghost! She was glowing and pulsing, clearly filled with anger. I'd been waiting for this moment to have my questions answered. But now that we were actually face to face, I was terrified. I realized I was holding my breath, and I didn't seem able to move.

This wasn't just the ghost of a girl who'd once been afraid of thunderstorms. This was a ghost that smashed glass figurines, broke dolls, ruined paintings, and destroyed precious family hand-me-downs like Peggy's mirror. I wanted to scream. But when I opened my mouth, no sound came out—just like Cassandra down in the yard.

My legs shook. Would they stop working just as my voice seemed to be doing? I imagined being somehow pulled into that blue light like dust into a vacuum cleaner.

I don't know how I did it, but suddenly, I was running and running. I practically flew down the stairs to my bedroom, then from there to the first floor, and finally out of the house. I heard the screen door slam shut behind me with a resounding bang. But even then I didn't stop. I kept running until I was standing in front of Cassandra Day.

"Who is that?" I demanded, staring up at Cassandra's wrinkled face. "You must tell me now!"

But she was still looking up at the tower room window, still shaking her head. I followed her gaze and saw just the window, as it always looked at that time of day.

"She isn't gone," Cassandra said softly. "She isn't going." Cassandra turned toward me and her eyes flashed. "Your hate is her fuel."

"Yes, yes, I know all that," I said impatiently. "But who is she?"

"What's going on out there?" Peggy yelled as she came out the back door. I turned away from Cassandra and watched Peggy striding quickly toward us.

I knew now who—or what—had broken Peggy's mirror. But I couldn't tell Peggy. She wouldn't believe anything I said about a ghost. It seemed that it was up to me now to get rid of it. But how?

I turned back to Cassandra to ask her. But she'd slipped away.

"Didn't I send you to your room, Diane?" Peggy demanded. She was just a few yards from me now and closing in fast.

"But.. but..." I stammered, searching for the right words. Had Peggy even seen Cassandra? Had she even really been there? I didn't know, and somehow it didn't seem to matter. What mattered now was getting rid of that thing up in my little room before it could do anything else to drive us all apart.

"No buts!" Peggy said. Her face was actually red with anger. "I want you to go back up there and stay up there until I say you can come down."

But I couldn't go back up, not now, not knowing what I knew about the ghost. I couldn't explain it to Peggy, either. About all I could do was run. That's just what I did. I ran and ran. Peggy tried to call me back, but I kept going.

Eleven

I ran through backyards until I got to the Reeds' house. I stopped on the back doorstep, a little out of breath. Frantically, I rang the doorbell. Thankfully, it was Stacey who came to the door. If she was still mad or hurt because of the stupid crack I'd made about her sounding like Peggy, it didn't show on her face.

"Hi," she said from the other side of the screen. Then she frowned as soon as she saw my face. "Wow, what is it? What's wrong?"

"Quick, Stacey!" I cried. "Let me in!" I looked nervously toward the bushes, expecting to see Peggy come bursting through them, prepared to drag me home.

Stacey yanked the screen door open and I hurried in. "What's up?" she asked.

Once I saw that we were alone in the Reeds' kitchen, I said, "I'm sorry, Stacey. I'm sorry about the stupid thing I said a little while ago. But mostly I'm sorry because...because I lied to you about the ghost. I thought I had to tell you what you wanted to hear or you wouldn't like me. I needed your friendship too much. That's why I did it."

"You're not making any sense, Diane," said Stacey. "You mean there really is a ghost?"

"Yes," I said. "It's true, I swear. But she isn't harmless like I thought she was. She's evil. I don't know who she is, but Cassandra does. Cassandra knows her and she's just as scared of her as I am. I have to get rid of her somehow. Until I do, I'm in danger. My whole family is in danger."

I stopped for a minute to search Stacey's face. "Do you believe me?" I asked.

Stacey seemed to think it over for a minute. Finally, she said, "Yes, I think I do. Why would you make something like this up?"

"I wouldn't," I assured her. "I couldn't. Will you help me, then?"

"What do you want me to do?" Stacey asked.

"I've got to find out who the ghost is," I said. "I've got to find out what she wants. If I can give her what she wants, she might just go away."

"How can we find out?" Stacey asked.

"Cassandra knows," I said, "but she won't

tell me for some reason. Maybe she's just too scared to tell me. I was thinking your mom might know since she knows a lot of local history."

Stacey shrugged. "She might."

"Is she home?" I asked.

Stacey nodded. "She's on the porch, I think."

Without waiting for Stacey to lead the way, I headed toward the porch. Stacey trailed after me.

"Hi, girls," Mrs. Reed said pleasantly. She was sitting at a glass-topped table. There were a lot of old photographs spread out in front of her. I decided she was probably working on one of her articles. "What can I do for you?" she asked.

Stacey stepped around me and said, "Diane's curious to know more about her old house, Mom. I told her that Cassandra Day used to live there. She's still hanging around over there, and they're all curious to know why."

Mrs. Reed nodded. "Poor old Cassandra," she said with a sigh. "What a long, hard life she's had."

"Did something happen in that house, Mrs. Reed?" I asked, trying not to sound as desperate and as frantic as I felt. "I mean, while

Cassandra was living there?"

Mrs. Reed seemed to hesitate before answering. Finally she said, "Well, I guess you girls are old enough to hear the story. Heaven knows, there are still enough rumors about it around this town, even though it happened more than 70 years ago."

Mrs. Reed shook her head slightly. "People can be so cruel sometimes, can't they?" she asked.

"Please, Mrs. Reed," I begged, feeling that my time was running out. "What happened?"

"Well, Cassandra's stepsister—a child named Anne Dorsey—fell from that tower room window and was killed. I read an old article at the historical society that said she broke her neck when she hit the ground."

"Was it an accident?" I asked breathlessly, even though I was sure I knew the answer.

"That's the saddest part of all," said Mrs. Reed. "Cassandra was up in that room when her stepsister fell to her death. And because the two girls never really got along, a lot of people believed Cassandra had pushed Anne out the window. But Cassandra was only Jenna's age."

"Lisa's age," I muttered. Then I asked, "How old was Cassandra's stepsister when this happened?"

"Twelve, I think. She'd just turned twelve not long before the accident. Quite a pretty girl, too, judging by the pictures," Mrs. Reed said.

"Did she do it?" Stacey asked. "Did Cassandra push her stepsister out the window?"

"Cassandra always claimed she was innocent," said Mrs. Reed. "She told police that Anne was responsible for her own death. She said what really happened was that Anne accidentally tumbled to her death while she was trying to push *Cassandra* out the window. There was a big investigation, but Cassandra was never brought to trial."

"Anne Dorsey," I said thoughtfully. That had to be the name of the tower room ghost, and I didn't want to forget it. Was the ghost angry because Cassandra hadn't been punished for causing her death? It made as much sense as anything else.

"That's right. Anne's father was the son of Dr. Dorsey, the man who built that house. If Dr. Dorsey had known that his only grandchild would die falling out of that tower, he probably would never have had it built," Mrs. Reed speculated. "But then, none of us can know the future, can we? Only the past. And some people—too many people, really—don't even bother to know that."

"What happened to Cassandra after the investigation?" I asked.

"Anne's father divorced Cassandra's mother. It was just too hard for them. I guess that after a tragedy like that, and not knowing who to blame, well...it's easy to understand. He sold the house and left town. I think he went to Chicago. Cassandra and her mother stayed in town. The mother's family was from here, I guess, even though none of them is around anymore. Anyway, Cassandra's mother died not long after the tragedy. Cassandra was passed along to one of her mother's relatives—a cousin, I think—but from what I understand she was never really wanted or loved. She stayed with the relative only until she was 14, and then went out on her own. It's no wonder she's a little crazy in her old age, is it? The poor soul," Mrs. Reed said.

"That's an awful story, Mom," Stacey said.

"Yes," Mrs. Reed agreed. "It is awful. But it explains why Cassandra can't seem to forget about that house. I think somewhere in that old mind of hers, she blames the house itself for her unhappy life. But that's how accidents are—sudden, random, unexplainable."

But I knew it wasn't the house Cassandra Day kept coming back to see. It was the ghost of Anne Dorsey. Had Cassandra actually pushed her older stepsister to her death? If she had, the ghost might be waiting up there to get revenge.

"Now," Mrs. Reed said, brightening. "Do you want me to tell you about the Morgans? They're the ones who bought the house from the Dorseys. He was a..."

But I cut her off. "No thanks, Mrs. Reed," I said, scrambling to my feet. "Maybe some other time. I have to get going now."

Stacey stood up, too. "I'll go with you," she said pointedly.

"Be back by five," Mrs. Reed called after us. "We're eating dinner early tonight. You're welcome to join us if you like, Diane."

"Thank you," I said. I couldn't tell her that I hoped to be battling a ghost by then.

"Where are we going now?" Stacey asked as soon as we were out of her mother's earshot. I was about to tell her when I heard the Reeds' telephone ring.

"Shh!" I said, pressing up against the wall, waiting to see who'd called, afraid it was Peggy. "Listen."

"Hello?" we heard Mrs. Reed say after the phone had rung three times. "Oh, I'm so glad to finally be talking to you, Peggy. Our girls have gotten to be such good friends in such a short time. I hope you'll consider coming..."

But Mrs. Reed didn't finish what I was sure had started out to be an invitation. Instead she said, "Why, yes. Both Diane and Stacey were in here with me just a few..."

I held my breath, listening. Then I heard Mrs. Reed say, "Of course. Just a minute." She put down the phone and I could hear her walking in the direction where we were hiding. She paused and called out, "Diane? Are you still here? It's Peggy, honey. She wants to talk to you."

"Shhh!" I ordered Stacey, putting a finger to my lips.

Mrs. Reed called out once more, then we heard the tap, tap, tap of her sandals as she returned to the phone. I took hold of Stacey's sleeve and pulled her toward the door.

"That was close," I said.

"What's going on?" Stacey asked after we'd slipped silently out the front door.

"Peggy's mad at me," I told her. "She thinks I broke her mirror. I thought Lisa did, but now I'm sure it was the ghost—Anne Dorsey. Anyway, Peggy's never going to believe that. She's sure I did it and wants me to stay in my room until I admit it and apologize."

"That's awful!" Stacey said.

I nodded. "That ghost thrives on making people fight with each other. She's been

115

making things around our house just awful. That's why I have to get rid of her," I explained as we hurried along Dorsey Avenue, away from the old Dorsey house and the evil ghost who possessed it.

"But how can you do that?" Stacey asked.

"I've got an idea about something that just might work," I told her. "That's why we're going to see Cassandra Day."

Stacey stopped walking. "What can that old woman do?" she demanded. "Won't she just make things even worse than they already are now?"

"Well, isn't a ghost just a restless spirit?" I asked Stacey. "The only way to get rid of it is to help it get rid of the reason for feeling restless. My guess is that Cassandra actually *did* kill her sister. Maybe it was an accident. Maybe it wasn't. But whatever happened up there that day, Anne Dorsey hasn't been able to rest quietly since. As Cassandra herself said, the ghost wants revenge."

"And you want to help the ghost get revenge?" Stacey asked, wide-eyed.

"Not exactly. What I'd like to do is bring Cassandra and the ghost together," I explained. "They might be able to reach some understanding that way. I'm sure they'd both be happier if they did. And then they'd both leave my family alone!"

"What if Cassandra can't do anything to help?" Stacey asked. "Or, what if she refuses?"

"I don't know," I answered, "but I have the awful feeling something terrible will happen. Someone will end up getting hurt or maybe even killed in that house. It's an angry ghost and will stop at nothing to get what it wants." The thought made me shudder.

"Can't you just move out?" Stacey asked. "Wouldn't that be easier?"

"Maybe," I agreed. "But how would I ever manage to talk Dad and Peggy into that? They love that house, Stacey, odd as that may seem. They're really proud of it."

"Okay," Stacey said. "I'll do what I can to help you."

"We've got to hurry," I said, picking up the pace. It helped to know Stacey was committed to my cause. "I have the terrible feeling Anne Dorsey will stop at nothing to get what she wants."

Twelve

W E'D gone almost three blocks when I realized I had no idea where Cassandra lived. Since she'd always come to our house on foot, I thought she probably lived close to our house. But there were busses running in Edmonton. Cassandra could have been taking a bus to and from Dorsey Avenue.

"Where does Cassandra live?" Stacey suddenly asked, as if reading my mind. I saw that we'd almost reached the part of town that mostly had businesses and stores.

"I was hoping you'd know," I admitted. But Stacey shook her head.

"There's a telephone booth at that gas station," I said, pointing a short distance away. "We'll look her address up."

But, when we tried that, we discovered that Cassandra Day wasn't listed.

"Maybe she doesn't have a phone," Stacey

suggested. She closed the phone book and set it back on a metal ledge in the telephone booth.

"Or maybe she just has an unlisted number," I said. "Either way, we're out of luck." Then I spotted the gas station attendant walking in our direction.

"What are you girls looking for?" he asked as we stepped away from the telephone booth. He was wiping his hands off on a rag that looked even dirtier than his hands. "Maybe I can help."

"An address," I told him cautiously.

He sorted of squinted at me and said, "Whose?"

"Someone named Cassandra Day," Stacey said. "Do you know where she lives?"

I gave her a funny look. Cassandra's house was hardly a landmark like the town hall or something. There was no reason for this man to know anything about Cassandra, much less where she lived.

But the attendant surprised me. "As a matter of fact, I sure do know where she lives," he said. Stacey shot me a triumphant look. The man pointed back up the street in the direction we'd come from.

"You go up there a block, then turn left and go another two blocks. She lives in an apartment building in the middle of the block," he said. "You can't miss it. Red brick, it is."

"You know her, then?" I asked stupidly.

"Everyone in this town knows that old gal," he said. Then he tapped the side of his head with his index finger. "She's not all there, you know. You girls better be careful."

"Thanks. We will," Stacey assured him. "We're not going to bother her or anything. We just have a message to deliver to her, that's all."

I was afraid he was going to ask what the message was, but he didn't. He just smiled in a neighborly way, then went on about his business.

"I never would have asked him that," I told Stacey as we hurried in the direction he'd told us to go.

"I know," she said. "That's why I came with you. You act tough, Diane, but I can tell you're not as tough as you think."

"Is that an insult?" I asked, ready to be offended.

"No, silly," Stacey said. "It's a compliment."

I knew right then that I had a new best friend. Knowing that made everything that was going on just a little bit easier to take.

"Is this it?" I asked Stacey a few minutes later. We'd reached an old, run-down brick apartment building.

"I think so," Stacey replied. Even though it was a hot August day, she hugged herself as if she were cold and shivered slightly. "Let's go inside and check the names on the mailboxes. Cassandra might not have a phone, but she's got to have a mailbox, right?"

"Right," I said, even though I wasn't any more sure of that than I was of anything else. Then I added, "Do you think she's home?" Now that we were here, I was almost tempted to go back. One word from Stacey, and I might have, ghost or no ghost.

"There's only one way for us to find out," Stacey said. She started up the front walk. I followed her.

The lobby was small, dingy, and filled with stale cooking odors. There was a single bare light bulb dangling from the ceiling and little piles of dust lay in the corners. Even the metal rows of mail slots looked forgotten.

"Ugh," I said. Stacey nodded in agreement. But she was already scanning the names over the mail slots.

"Here!" she cried when she found it. "She's in apartment 206. That must be on the second floor."

We opened a scarred door off the lobby that led to a stairwell. Slowly, we climbed grimy, linoleum stairs. Just as we reached the second floor, I started hearing angry voices. As we got closer and closer to 206, Cassandra's apartment, the angry voices got louder and louder. Then I realized they were coming from 206!

"She isn't alone," I whispered to Stacey as we inched closer. "I thought she'd be alone."

"What should we do now?" Stacey asked softly.

"I don't know," I confessed. I thought about turning back, but I knew it was too late for that. I took a deep breath, lifted my fist, and started to pound on Cassandra's door.

Abruptly, the voices stopped. I heard cautious footsteps headed toward the door. The footsteps stopped, and the next sound was that of the door being unlocked. Slowly, the door opened a crack.

"Yes?" asked a creaky voice through the crack.

"Cassandra?" I asked, not knowing what else to call her.

"What do you want?" she demanded, her tone changing.

"I want to talk to you about Anne," I said, "Anne Dorsey, your stepsister."

The door snapped quickly shut, and I thought I'd lost my only hope. Cassandra wasn't even going to talk to me, despite the warnings that she'd seemed so big on giving me. But just as I was about to tell Stacey that we might as well go home, Cassandra's door opened all the way.

"Come in," she said. "I guess I shouldn't be surprised to see you."

Stacey and I looked at each other briefly. I was trying to decide whether we should run. Stacey had to be thinking the same thing. We could see Cassandra, but had no idea who had been arguing with her inside. We held back for a moment or two, but finally followed Cassandra inside.

The shades were drawn, and there was a weird, throbbing glow coming from the corner of the room. My palms began to sweat. The hair stood up on my arms.

And then I realized what I was seeing. *The television!* I thought, feeling like an idiot. The loud voices we'd heard arguing had come from the TV! Cassandra had been alone after all.

Cassandra hurried over and switched the set off. "So now you believe me, do you?" she asked when she came back. Her eyes were focused on me alone.

"I know now what happened to your stepsister," I said. "I also know she's haunting the tower room."

Cassandra nodded. "She's been up there all these years, waiting. I used to think she was waiting for me. I'd see her up there, but no one else would. When I told people about it, they said it was guilt that made me see her. But I knew I had nothing to feel guilty about, except maybe hating her. If I hadn't hated her, though, it would have been me lying dead on the ground that afternoon."

I sneaked a look at Stacey. Her face was pale. I didn't have to look in a mirror to know mine was, too.

"You see," Cassandra continued, "I never trusted Anne. She never let me up there. It was her room, she said, and I couldn't come in. She couldn't be talked into letting me in. But then, that one day, she suddenly changed her mind. Suddenly, she *wanted* me up there. Well, of course she did! She wanted to push me out!"

Cassandra's eyes narrowed. She leaned forward in her seat. "I went up. I went into her little tower room. But I kept my eye on her," Cassandra said, "and it was a good thing, too. I saw her coming with her arms up, all set to push. Just in time, I stepped aside. Out she went! I watched her fall. Then they saw me up there, and said I'd done it. No one would listen to me. Not then, not ever."

I realized I'd been holding my breath, listening to Cassandra tell about that one awful day. "What...what happened next?" I asked quietly.

"Well, she made my life awful," Cassandra replied. "She would break things of mine, and get me in trouble with every adult who had ever known us. They were always on her side when she was alive, and she made sure they stayed on her side when she was dead. No matter what went wrong, I got blamed. That's why I got away from people as soon as I could. I was only 14 when I struck out on my own, but I knew I'd be better off alone than around other people. They'd all grown to hate me. Anne had made sure of that. And she's too spiteful to give up, to rest like she should. She's a bad one. She always was, too."

Cassandra lifted her blue eyes and I saw that she was actually crying.

"I believe you," I said softly. "I know what she can do. She's been doing awful things to me and my family, too. And everyone blames me! Will you help us? We have to get rid of her, but I don't think we can without you."

But Cassandra shook her old head. "Anne was evil—still *is* evil. I warned your folks that she was in there and that she was waiting for a family just like yours. But they wouldn't listen to me, either. Now I'm afraid it's too late. Anne won't stop until she gets what she wants."

"What *does* she want?" I asked. "I want her to have whatever it is. I want her to stop."

Cassandra's wrinkled old face clouded over. "What did she ever want? Attention, I thought. She hated to have me get anything from anyone, even a smile, especially if it came from her father." Cassandra laughed, a little sadly. "Well, you'd think she'd be satisfied with ruining my life and my mother's life as well. But she'll never be satisfied. No, not her."

"Please," I begged, "tell me what she wants!"

"Isn't it obvious?" Cassandra asked. "Can't you guess?"

"No," I said wildly. "Tell me!"

"She wants me to go back up there. She wants to finish what she meant to do."

I gasped. "You don't mean...?"

Cassandra nodded. "She wants to push *me* out of that window. She wants to see *my* broken body lying on the lawn right where hers was found."

"But why is she bothering *us?*" I asked.

"Because you came to her, my dear. You came into her little room, and you loved it like

126

she did," Cassandra said. She paused for a minute. "And now you've come here to ask for my help. You wanted to ask me to go back with you, to go up there, to help you get rid of her."

"Yes!" I cried. "Please! Will you?"

But Cassandra said, "No. I will never set foot in that house again. I owe you nothing. I've already given you more than you deserve. I've seen you with your own stepsister. You're as awful as Anne was."

"But I thought Lisa was to blame for all the broken things," I protested. "I didn't know it was Anne."

"It doesn't matter to me," Cassandra said. Her voice sounded bitter. "I've done all I'm willing to do for you already. I warned your father and stepmother, and I warned you. Don't move in there, I said. Not with children. Especially not with two girls, two stepsisters. It was too much for Anne's spirit. Your restlessness made her restless. Now you tell me that you're sorry. But you're too late, aren't you?"

"Come on, Diane," Stacey said. She looked angry. "You're not going to get any help here. We're just wasting our time. She's as rotten as she claims Anne was. She may not have pushed Anne, but she was glad Anne fell."

Stacey grabbed my hand and pulled me toward Cassandra's apartment door.

"Wait," Cassandra called before Stacey could open the door.

I turned back. "Have you changed your mind? Will you go with us?" I asked eagerly.

But Cassandra said, "No, I won't do that. I can't. But I do have a suggestion. It might not work, but you can try."

Stacey started pulling on me again, but I took my hand away from her.

"What?" I asked. "I'll try anything."

"You must give up the tower room yourself. Don't let anyone else go up there, either. Keep the door locked and stay out," Cassandra advised.

"But locked doors don't keep ghosts in," I protested. "What good will locking the door do?"

"Anne was a spoiled, stubborn girl when my mother married her father," Cassandra explained. "Her own mother died when she was born and her father gave her anything and everything to make it up to her. When he had to be away on business, Anne would throw horrible tantrums and break anything she could find. The more cherished the thing was, the more Anne enjoyed breaking it."

I thought of my glass goose girl, Lisa's favorite doll, Peggy's mirror, and my painting. I shuddered. Somehow, Anne had guessed how important each of those things was to its owner. That was why she'd broken them.

"My mother tried reasoning with Anne," explained Cassandra. "But Anne wouldn't be reasoned with. Finally, my mother took to locking her in that tower room, more to contain her rages than to punish her, really."

"And did it work?" I asked.

Cassandra nodded. "Anne would quiet down whenever she was locked in, probably so Mother would unlock the door again...which, of course, she always did. You see, that's all Mother wanted—peace and quiet. We could have been a happy family, the four of us together. But Anne ruined that chance, too."

"I'm going to try it," I said, reaching up to touch the skeleton key that hung safely around my neck. I didn't know if a locked door would keep Anne in, but it was the only chance I might have. And maybe it *would* work. After all, when Anne was a child she had grown to see the locked tower door as some sort of barrier that she couldn't penetrate. Stubborn as she was, Anne's will hadn't been as strong as Cassandra's mother's. She wasn't allowed out of the tower room until Cassandra's mother was good and ready to let her out. Maybe my will now would be stronger than Anne's.

I backed toward the door. Stacey was holding it open, and I spun around and hurried out into the hall with her. Cassandra followed us as far as the door and closed it after us.

Stacey and I raced down the stairs and out of the apartment building. As we started home, I couldn't help wondering what I was going to do if Cassandra's suggestion didn't work. *But it would work,* I told myself firmly as Stacey and I walked down the street in stunned silence. It would work because it had to work.

Thirteen

"WANT me to come home with you?" Stacey asked, finally breaking our silence when we'd reached our block of Dorsey Avenue.

"No," I said. "I better go home alone." I had to face Peggy now, and it wasn't going to be easy.

When we got to Stacey's house, Stacey said a quick good-bye and hurried inside. I went on alone.

The big, old house looked quiet and threatening as I got closer to it. *What*, I wondered, *would I find inside?* The porch creaked as I crossed it, and the front door squeaked eerily as I opened it.

"Hello?" I said slowly, not knowing what to expect.

"Diane!" Peggy came rushing out of the kitchen and, to my surprise, hugged me. "I've been so worried. Are you all right? I thought you'd run away!"

"I'm all right," I said, embarrassed. "And I'm sorry I ran off like that."

Peggy stopped hugging me and pulled back. I could see that her worry was being replaced with some of the anger she'd been feeling earlier. I wondered what I would say if she brought up the broken mirror again. I knew I couldn't tell her a ghost had broken it, even though that's what I now believed.

"You missed lunch," Peggy said. I guess she had decided not to bring up the mirror, at least not now. "Would you like me to fix you something?" she asked. "Are you hungry?"

"Not very," I said. Then, out of the corner of my eye, I caught some movement. It was her! It was Anne. If I hadn't known about her, hadn't been tuned into her, I might have missed her altogether. She was so wispy and airy that she was almost not there. My mouth dropped open.

"What's wrong?" Peggy asked. Her eyes searched my face. "Are you sure you're all right?" As I watched, the ghost floated up the stairs.

"Uh...yes," I said when I could no longer see Anne's ghost. "I'm all right." I looked back at Peggy. "Where is Lisa?" I asked.

"She's over at Jenna's house," Peggy said. "Why?"

"No reason," I said, shrugging. "I guess maybe I don't feel well, after all. I'm going to go lie down."

I took a deep breath, then edged away and followed the path Anne had taken up the stairs. I had to do it now. I had to lock the door to my little room while I was certain she was up there. Otherwise, I might be locking her out instead of in.

"What about lunch?" Peggy called after me.

"No, thank you," I said. "I'm not hungry." I could feel Peggy watching me curiously as I continued to climb the steps, but I was determined now not to stop.

I reached the top of the stairs just in time to see Anne Dorsey's ghost float into my bedroom. There was something cold and sinister about the way she moved. I wondered just what she'd been up to downstairs. Probably something horrible. I shuddered. I didn't want to be following her even now. I wanted to run and keep running. But I had no choice. This ghost was getting bolder and bolder by the minute. She had to be stopped. I hurried after her as quickly and as quietly as I could.

When I reached the door to my bedroom, I saw the last wisp of pale blue light move up the narrow staircase to the little tower room above. I didn't waste a second. I dashed across the bedroom and slammed the door. My heart was pounding as I ripped the key from my neck. Quickly, I locked the door. *Did I imagine it,* I asked myself, *or had there actually been an angry scream from above?*

"Diane!" I heard Peggy calling to me from below. "What's going on up there?"

"Nothing," I called back. I hoped my voice sounded normal. But now something was clawing at the other side of the door.

"You're not getting out!" I told the ghost as fiercely as I could. I hoped my voice would remind her of the times she had been locked in there as a child, and that the command alone would keep her from trying too hard to escape. "You might as well give up and quiet down. You can stay up there for eternity if you want. But I'm not going to let you out."

The pounding grew louder.

What would happen, I wondered, *when the banging grew loud enough for Peggy to hear?* Before I could find out, though, the banging suddenly stopped. I heard a long, drawn-out sigh. It was like a strong wind pushing its way through tall pines. Then everything got quiet.

I sighed gratefully. Then, feeling exhausted from all I'd been through, I walked to my bed and lay down. I closed my eyes, and soon I fell into a deep and thankfully dreamless sleep.

When I woke up later, I thought it was night already. Then I realized that it was only early afternoon. The sky had clouded up, and it was about to storm. I thought about going up to watch the storm through my skylight. But of course, it took me only a second to remember what was up there. *I could never look up through that skylight again,* I told myself sadly.

There was a flash of lightning, followed closely by a loud clap of thunder. The wind kicked up, and I could hear it tearing at the trees outside. I heard a soft moan. Then, after the next clap of thunder, I heard a louder moan. It was coming from my little tower room. I got up and walked to the locked door.

"So," I called through the door. "You *are* afraid of storms, aren't you?"

I heard the ghost of Anne Dorsey moan again. It was a pitiful sound, a little like the wind, but more lonely, and more pitiful. I felt sorry for the ghost for a second. I thought about how awful it must have been when she was locked up there as a child. But then I remembered she'd been locked up there to contain her rages. And I remembered all the awful things she had done to me.

"It won't work," I said stubbornly. "I'm not unlocking that door for you. Not now, not ever."

I turned away and left the room. I found Peggy and Lisa downstairs, watching TV. I joined them. For the first time since coming to Edmonton, I enjoyed their company.

* * * * *

"Is it working?" Stacey whispered. The ghost of Anne Dorsey had been locked in my little tower room for three days. As far as I knew, she hadn't gotten out, either.

"Sort of," I whispered back. "But I still wish there was some way to get rid of her forever. She's really noisy. She's driving me nuts."

I told Stacey how the ghost banged and rattled around a lot. She also moaned and cried. But no one seemed to hear her except me. I should have been relieved, I guess. And I was, in one way. But, in another way, I felt like I was starting to go crazy myself.

Peggy, Lisa, and I were at the Reeds' for a backyard barbecue. Dad was still out of town and wouldn't be back for another week yet. Mr. Reed was cooking chicken. Peggy and Mrs. Reed were sitting at the Reeds' picnic table, sipping iced tea and chatting about wallpaper. Lisa and Jenna were trying to set up the badminton set that Mr. Reed had dragged out. So far, Stacey and I had resisted helping them.

We watched the younger girls for a while, then turned our conversation back to the ghost.

"So the lock keeps her in?" Stacey asked.

I nodded. "It seems to. Nothing's been broken or damaged since I locked her in. But like I said, I sure do hear her up there, especially at night when she wakes me up," I complained.

"It's hard to believe no one else hears her carrying on," Stacey commented.

I shrugged. "I know. But I don't think anyone does. At least, they don't mention it if they do." I saw that Lisa and Jenna were on their way over, so I motioned for Stacey to be quiet.

"Help us," Jenna insisted. "We aren't tall enough to hang the net."

"Go away," Stacey told her.

"Oh, come on," I said to Stacey. "We can play them a game after we get the net up." Stacey gave me a questioning look, then stood up. We headed over to the badminton net.

Ever since I'd locked Anne Dorsey's ghost

in my little room, I'd been trying my best to be as nice as possible to Lisa. For one thing, I knew now that some of the things I'd been blaming her for weren't her fault. I felt pretty guilty about being so unfair. But also, whenever she seemed really whiny or demanding, I'd try to remember what it had been like for me when I was eight years old. Usually, that worked. I'd be more patient then. And eventually, Lisa would settle down, too.

The four of us worked together to put up the net. The first game we played was Stacey and I against Lisa and Jenna. We were all pretty terrible, but Stacey and I caught on faster than Lisa and Jenna. Eventually, we beat them. Then Stacey and Lisa went up against Jenna and I. Stacey and Lisa won that one. When we switched again, Lisa and I were on the same side and we won.

"I must be the best," Lisa crowed. Not long ago, hearing her brag like that would have made me mad. But now I agreed.

"That's sure the way it looks," I told her, giving one of her blond braids a tug.

"Dinner!" Mr. Reed yelled. He was holding a platter of chicken that looked as delicious as it smelled. I smiled. I was actually having fun with Lisa around. I decided I might even be having more fun *because* Lisa was around.

I caught her looking at me, and I smiled. Lisa must have known that my smile was genuine, because she smiled back.

Later, Peggy, Lisa, and I walked home through the backyards separating the Reeds' from our own house. As we came through the hedge that Peggy had finally trimmed the day before, I couldn't help glancing up at the tower room window. I was hoping what I'd been hoping since I locked the door to my little room—that the ghost of Anne Dorsey had given up her quest to get even and had finally gone wherever it is spirits are supposed to finally rest.

But there she was, perfectly framed by the tower room window, glowing that ghastly blue I'd come to dread. I knew she was looking back at me, too. And though her eyes were too far away for me to see, I knew they were filled with hate. She'd tried to get my help. She'd thought I was like her. She'd thought I was filled with the same kind of selfishness and hate. But she'd been wrong, and now I was as much her enemy as old Cassandra Day.

Finally, I managed to tear my eyes away from the sight. I looked over at Peggy. Had she seen the ghost? Could she see the ghost? But she wasn't even looking up. She was looking down instead, down at the flower bed she'd weeded earlier in the day.

"Won't your father be pleased when he comes home?" she asked. She bent down to sniff some yellow mums.

"Yes," I said, though I wasn't really listening. My mind was on my dilemma. Should I tell Peggy about the ghost? I thought I trusted her enough by now to try it. But did she trust me enough to believe me if she couldn't see the ghost herself? So far, no one had been able to see Anne's ghost except Cassandra and I. Why that was, I didn't know. I just knew that it was.

"I want an ice cream cone," Lisa said, skipping ahead and disappearing through the back screen door.

"How about you, Diane?" Peggy asked. She draped her arm across my shoulders. The closeness felt good.

"Sure," I said, nestled against her side and matching my stride to hers as we got closer to the back door. "That sounds great."

Fourteen

"**P**LEASE?" Lisa begged again. She wanted to go up in the tower. It was afternoon and we were both watching TV in the living room. Peggy had gone to a seminar on bathroom remodeling, and I was baby-sitting for her.

"No," I said. "You can't go up there." I'd already told Lisa twice that she couldn't go to my little room, but she refused to give up. I had no one to blame except myself, either. I'd been too nice to Lisa lately. Now she thought I'd give in if she asked me long and hard enough.

"Please?" she asked again. "I won't hurt anything. I promise." She slid closer to me on the couch, looking up at me with her big, blue-green eyes.

"No!" I said again. "I don't even go up anymore. It's too hot up there this time of year."

"But it's not hot today. It's nice," Lisa said.

"You still can't," I said.

"Why not?" Lisa demanded.

I scrambled for some reason that might satisfy her. "Because there's a squirrel trapped up there," I said. "My dad will have to get it out when he gets home. Squirrels can have rabies, you know."

Lisa edged away from me, her lower lip slowly coming out in a pout.

"You're making that up, Diane. I know you are. There's no squirrel up there, or Mom would have called someone out about it the way she did when we had a mouse in our apartment once."

I reached over and flipped off the TV. It was a rerun I'd already seen twice before, anyway. Neither of us was really watching it.

"Think of something else you'd like to do," I told Lisa, hoping to distract her. "I'll do it with you."

"I don't want to do anything else," she said stubbornly.

"I'll play a game with you," I offered. "I'll play any one you want to play, too. Even that dumb one with the timer and the shark."

Lisa shook her head. "I don't want to play a game. I want to go up in your little room.

You never let me up there," she complained. "You're selfish."

I looked at her, wondering what she'd say if she knew the truth. She'd be terrified, that's what. I was protecting Lisa, but Lisa didn't know it. How long was I going to be able to go on keeping it from her? What would Peggy and Dad say when she finally went to them to complain about my little room? Then what was I going to say to them? Were they all going to demand to go up? What would the ghost do then?

Suddenly, the doorbell rang. Thankful for the distraction, I got up and went to see who was there. It was Stacey.

"Come in," I said, practically pulling her through the door. "You're just in time. I could really use your help."

"For what?" she asked.

But instead of answering Stacey, I turned to say something to Lisa about calling Jenna and inviting her over, too. I was going to suggest that the four of us play that awful shark game Lisa liked so much. But Lisa had left the room.

"She was right here a second ago. Oh, well," I said, flipping the TV back on and collapsing on the couch. "I guess she found something else to do."

Stacey looked quickly around. "Who are you talking about?" she asked nervously. I couldn't help chuckling. Stacey had never seen the ghost, but our visit to Cassandra's apartment had convinced her that it existed.

"Lisa, of course," I told her. Stacey looked relieved.

"What are you watching?" she asked, flopping down on the couch next to me.

I sighed. "Reruns. I can't wait until the new shows start in a couple of weeks. It's too bad my dad refuses to hook up to cable. He won't even let us have a VCR."

Stacey gave me a sympathetic look and then slumped deeper into the couch. We'd both begun to feel lazy from watching when there was a loud banging on the front door. I yawned, then went to see who was there.

Pulling open the door, I was shocked to see Cassandra Day standing there. She was wild-eyed and seemed to be out of breath.

"What's wrong?" I demanded, suddenly alert. But Cassandra pushed past me without bothering to answer. She seemed to know just where she was going. But then, the house should be familiar to her. After all, she'd lived here before, even if it was just for a short time decades ago. What was odd was that she'd come in at all. I knew the house terrified her, and I knew why, too.

"What is it?" I asked, hurrying after her. Cassandra was charging up the stairs to the second floor now and wasn't to be stopped. Her age didn't seem to slow her down much.

"Something is wrong!" she said without turning around. "Something is terribly wrong!"

I felt a prickle of fear and ran faster. Stacey was close behind me. With sure steps, Cassandra rushed down the hall toward my bedroom. I heard her old lady shoes start up the steps to my little tower room just as I reached the bedroom door myself.

"Oh, no, Diane!" Stacey gasped as she followed me into my room. "That crazy old woman has unlocked the door! The ghost will escape. How can we stop it?" But I knew Stacey was wrong. Cassandra Day hadn't unlocked the door. She hadn't had time. Lisa must have. But how? Touching the spot around my neck where my key usually hung from a string, I discovered with a shock that the key was gone. Then I saw it. It was stuck in the door. The string had broken. *It must have fallen off of me, and Lisa must have found it,* I thought. When I wouldn't go along with her, she got mad. She'd gone up there to show me up...it was just the kind of angry act I now knew the ghost fed upon. Suddenly, I heard a piercing scream. Then I heard Lisa's terrified voice.

"Please! Please! Don't touch me! Don't come near me," she was screaming. "Go away! Let me alone! Mommy! Diane! Somebody! Help!"

I took the steps two at a time, my heart pounding. I gasped when I saw poor little Lisa backing slowly toward the window. It was wide open. Lisa's eyes were bigger than I'd ever seen them, and they were filled with terror. But then I saw that it wasn't the ghost that had Lisa so frightened. I don't think Lisa had even noticed the ghost yet. Lisa was terrified of wild-eyed Cassandra.

But *I* saw the ghost of Anne Dorsey there, on the other side of the room. I saw what Cassandra saw. The ghost was drifting slowly toward Lisa, and I was positive that it meant to harm her. A cold, icy wind was whipping around the room now, despite how nice it was outside.

"Lisa, stop!" I ordered her. "Don't move!" But if Lisa heard me, my words weren't getting through to her. All of her attention was focused on Cassandra. Even though I knew Cassandra meant only to save her, Lisa didn't know that. All she knew was that the old woman who had been frightening her for weeks was coming straight at her. And she was scared to death.

"I'm here now, Anne," I heard Cassandra mutter, as she moved closer and closer toward Lisa. "You've got me where you want me. You can leave these people alone now. It's me you want, not them."

The ghost of Anne Dorsey hung in midair for a moment, as if trying to decide something. Then she turned away from Lisa and started floating toward Cassandra. Meanwhile, Lisa was acting more and more frantic. She continued backing toward that open window in a panic. I knew I had to get to Lisa soon or she would surely fall.

"No!" Lisa whimpered over and over again. "No!"

I tried to get past Cassandra, but the ghost was blocking my way and I couldn't bring myself to actually push through her.

"No!" I heard again. But this time it came from Cassandra, and not Lisa. I never would have thought it was possible considering how old she was, but Cassandra was suddenly moving toward Lisa at a speed I don't think I ever could have managed. Her spindly arms were held out, as if to catch Lisa.

Unfortunately, even though I knew what Cassandra meant to do, Lisa didn't. Scrambling backward even faster than she had been before, Lisa was now just inches from the low window. I held my breath, terrified that Lisa would fall to her death and I would be powerless to stop it. I began to move toward Lisa, even though I knew I would never reach her in time.

But then the ghost pulsed brightly—more brightly than ever—and flashed across the room like a blue streak of lightning. It reached Lisa before Cassandra or I could. Helplessly, I clamped my eyes shut, feeling that all I could do now was avoid seeing that terrible moment when Lisa would tumble out the window. Or maybe the ghost would actually push her out. I waited to hear Lisa scream as she fell to her death. But I heard nothing in those long seconds. There were no final screams. Slowly, I dared to open my eyes.

The first thing I saw was Lisa lying in the corner of the room, her face buried in her hands. She was sobbing, but safe. I rushed to her and held her tight.

"It's okay," I told her, smoothing back the rumpled remains of her blond braids. "I'm here now. It's okay. I won't let anything hurt you."

"Is that what you meant to do?" I heard Cassandra ask. Her voice sounded soft, and amazed. I looked up and saw that she was talking to the ghost of Anne Dorsey. The ghost looked small and child-like as it faced the old woman.

"You meant to *save* me from falling all those many years ago?" Cassandra continued. "But I thought you meant to push me. I leaped aside, and then you fell."

Slowly, the ghost nodded her wispy blue head, and I thought I could hear her say, "Yes, oh, yes. I never meant to hurt you."

"You've waited and waited just to tell me that, haven't you?" Cassandra asked. Her voice was hoarse and her eyes were glistening with tears. And I felt a great sadness. So much time had been wasted. So many lives had been lonely for no reason. And it had all been just a terrible mistake. It seemed so unfair.

"All this time I thought you hated me, but you didn't," said Cassandra. "You loved me, didn't you? All these years...all the things you've done...you've only been trying to get my attention—and now the attention of Diane—to let me know how frustrated you've been that I didn't understand. You never meant any real harm."

The ghost of Anne Dorsey nodded again. She was shrinking, I realized, and fading slowly away. Soon, it would be hard to see her image at all.

Now, Cassandra lifted her arms and held them out to the little ghost. "Come," she said. "Let's forgive each other. It's time to forgive."

Cassandra began to smile. Through my own tears, I smiled too. As I watched, with Lisa sheltered in my arms, Anne Dorsey drifted into Cassandra's open arms. The glow the ghost gave off was gentle now, and it seemed to settle all around the old woman. Finally, Cassandra's thin arms closed gently around the ghost in a loving hug.

"Good-bye," Cassandra said, her voice a whisper. "Good-bye, dear sister." The blue glow grew fainter and fainter until there was nothing left to be seen. Cassandra stood there quietly, her face peaceful now.

"Oh, wow!" I heard Stacey exclaim. Turning around, I saw Stacey standing on the top step. Her face was white. I could tell from her expression that she'd seen the ghost and most, if not all, of what had happened up there. It *had* really happened. Hard as it was to believe, all of it had really happened. And now it was finally over

"I'm home!" I heard Peggy yell from the first floor. "Where is everybody?"

I looked down at Lisa. She was wiping her eyes with the back of her hand.

"What just happened up here is our secret, right?" I asked softly. I knew Lisa and Stacey had just seen what I did.

Lisa nodded. "Right."

"Right," Stacey agreed. "No one would believe us if we told them, anyway."

Then I looked at Cassandra Day. How was I going to get her out of the house without letting Peggy see her? I wasn't. I'd have to think of a good story to tell Peggy, one that she would be able to believe. Somehow, I knew I could do it. After what we'd just been through, I felt like I could do anything.

Fifteen

AFTER that hot August day when Cassandra finally came back up to the little room and faced Anne Dorsey's ghost, there was no more terror in our house...no cold drafts, no odd whispers, no strange lights or terrified cries in the night. Now I could let Lisa up in my studio. Well, *sometimes* I'd let her up there, as long as I wasn't working on a project.

By the time school started in September, the whole crazy thing began to seem more like a dream than a memory. As time went on and nothing weird happened, Peggy grew to trust me. Once, I overheard her explain to Dad that she'd been a little hard on me, that she'd tried to rush things. And even though she never found out how her mirror got broken, she even apologized for accusing me of doing it! We were all getting along like I knew Dad had wanted, and it felt good. It felt right.

Edmonton Junior High turned out to be as great as Stacey had said it would be. Luckily, we had several classes together and ate during the same lunch period. I made a lot of new friends right away, but Stacey continued to be my best friend.

A couple of times, Stacey, Lisa, Jenna, and I went to visit Cassandra Day. We knew now that she wasn't an awful old woman. She'd been lonely and frightened, that was all. Those times we'd stop over, she'd give us lemonade and cookies, and we'd talk. We never talked about that strange day, though. I think we all wondered if it had really happened. I know I did, anyway.

Then, in October, Gran finally came for a visit. It was her birthday, and we were going to help her celebrate. We'd planned the party for Sunday evening. We were going to have Gran's favorite, baked chicken, and a big birthday cake.

"Let's invite some other people to the party," Lisa suggested the Saturday morning Gran was due to arrive on the bus from Springfield.

"Exactly who are you thinking of, honey?" Peggy asked.

"The Reeds," Lisa said.

Dad set down the newspaper he'd been reading and nodded. "That's a good idea, Lisa. I'm sure Gran would enjoy meeting them."

"And Cassandra Day," Lisa added quickly. Peggy gasped, and Lisa and I exchanged quick looks.

"Cassandra Day and Diane's grandmother are probably the same age," Lisa said. "Maybe they could be friends."

"I think inviting Cassandra Day is a good idea, too," I said, backing Lisa up. "If Gran makes some friends here ahead of time, she might consider moving to Edmonton sometime." I sneaked a peek at Dad and he seemed to be considering the idea.

But Peggy was shaking her head. "I don't know," she said. "I'm not crazy about the idea. Cassandra hasn't come by to stare at the house since the day you girls let her in when I wasn't home. I hate to encourage her strange visits again."

"She won't do that anymore. I'm sure of it," I said to Peggy. "She just wanted to see what things looked like inside after all those years when she lived here herself."

I'd said the same thing to her the day Cassandra had finally confronted the ghost of Anne Dorsey. But, just as she had that day,

Peggy looked like she didn't quite believe me. I didn't really blame her, since it wasn't really the truth.

"I like Cassandra Day," Lisa said. "She's a nice person, and she's lonely. I bet she hasn't been to a birthday party for ages, either." Even Peggy had to laugh at that.

"I don't think it would hurt anything, Peg," Dad said at last. "Maybe Cassandra Day has some interesting stories about the house she'll decide to tell us."

"I think I'd just as soon *not* hear any 'interesting' stories that Cassandra might have about this house, thank you just the same," said Peggy, chuckling. "But all right. If you girls want to invite her for dinner tomorrow, go ahead," she said.

And that's how Cassandra Day happened to be sitting in our yard the next evening with the four Reeds, Gran, and the four of us. She seemed like any other old woman now, and not at all like the crazy person she'd been when I'd first met her. Cassandra and Gran talked about the old days when they were children, and we listened. Baked chicken turned out to be Cassandra's favorite dish, too. Peggy looked constantly surprised that Cassandra was so pleasant.

When the cake arrived later, Cassandra

asked Gran how old she was. Without hesitating a second, Gran told her.

"That's the age my stepsister would be now," Cassandra said wistfully. "It's funny, but being four years apart in age seemed like so many years when we were children." She looked thoughtfully at Gran. "But now it wouldn't matter, really, just as it doesn't when you and I are talking. It feels like we're exactly the same age."

Gran nodded and said, "That's right, Cassie, my dear—old."

All the grown-ups chuckled at that, all of them except Cassandra herself. Instead, she glanced up at the tower room window as if expecting to see something. Both Stacey and I glanced quickly up there, too. But there was nothing in the tower room window now, nothing but the reflection of the setting sun. The spirit of Anne Dorsey had finally found peace. At the same time, I knew that she'd always be a part of that house...and always a part of me, too.

About the Author

LAURIE LYKKEN has always loved pretending. "Being a professional writer gives me a legitimate excuse to continue pretending the way I did as a child, even though I'm grown up now," Laurie says.

She lives in Minnesota with her husband Bruce and their two young sons, Nate and Zach. Laurie and her family enjoy biking, swimming, fishing, canoeing, sailing, skiing, skating, and reading together.

"I get my best ideas during solitary, early morning walks," says Laurie. "I find coming up with ideas is a lot like fishing. Not every idea I have is a keeper. But if I'm patient with myself and keep throwing that line out there, I know I'll eventually hook something worth hanging on to and developing."

Laurie has worked at a variety of jobs, from teaching preschool to writing computer manuals. Her favorite job, however, is writing books for children and young adults.

Laurie has had 14 books for children and for young adults published. *Little Room of Terror* is her first book for Willowisp Press.